PRAISE FOR
CARLTON MELLICK III

"Easily the craziest, weirdest, strangest, funniest, most obscene writer in America."
—*GOTHIC MAGAZINE*

"Carlton Mellick III has the craziest book titles... and the kinkiest fans!"
—CHRISTOPHER MOORE, author of *The Stupidest Angel*

"If you haven't read Mellick you're not nearly perverse enough for the twenty first century."
—JACK KETCHUM, author of *The Girl Next Door*

"Carlton Mellick III is one of bizarro fiction's most talented practitioners, a virtuoso of the surreal, science fictional tale."
—CORY DOCTOROW, author of *Little Brother*

"Bizarre, twisted, and emotionally raw—Carlton Mellick's fiction is the literary equivalent of putting your brain in a blender."
—BRIAN KEENE, author of *The Rising*

"Carlton Mellick III exemplifies the intelligence and wit that lurks between its lurid covers. In a genre where crude titles are an art in themselves, Mellick is a true artist."
—*THE GUARDIAN*

"Just as Pop had Andy Warhol and Dada Tristan Tzara, the bizarro movement has its very own P. T. Barnum-type practitioner. He's the mutton-chopped author of such books as *Electric Jesus Corpse* and *The Menstruating Mall*, the illustrator things bizarro, and his name is Carlton
—*DETAILS MAGAZINE*

D1453374

Also by
Carlton Mellick III

NEVERDAY

CARLTON MELLICK III

ERASERHEAD PRESS

PORTLAND, OREGON

ERASERHEAD PRESS
P.O. BOX 10065
PORTLAND, OR 97296

WWW.ERASERHEADPRESS.COM

ISBN: 978-1-62105-264-7

Printed in the USA.

AUTHOR'S NOTE

Like my novel *Quicksand House*, *Neverday* was a concept I had in my head for a decade or two before I finally fleshed it out into a book. I always loved Groundhog Day-style time loop stories and always felt that there was so much unexplored territory to play with. Lately, there's been a re-emergence of films that play with this trope—*Edge of Tomorrow*, *Repeaters*, *Naked*, and *Happy Death Day*. I thought it was about time to do my own take, but I wanted to do a story where it's not just one person repeating the same day over and over again. I wanted to explore what it would be like if almost everyone in the world was stuck in the same situation and how society would adapt to living in a world without a progression of time. *Neverday* is the result.

This is one of the only books that I didn't write marathon-style. Usually, I check into a hotel or beach house and write a book nonstop from beginning to end in one go. This time I tried taking my time and spreading the work out over a much longer period than just a week or two. I'm not sure if the results are any different as far as quality is concerned. I'll let you be the judge of that. Personally, I've always thought that writers who prefer to "take their time" are really just looking for an excuse to procrastinate. I'm not sure that's always true, but I personally prefer to set out with a more ambitious work ethic. Neverday was kind of a cross between the two—I worked the same amount of hours per day as I normally do while marathon-writing but I only wrote about 500 words a day rather than 500 words an hour. I hope the extra attention to detail pays off for you… or maybe it won't make much of a difference. Either way, I hope you enjoy it.

—Carlton Mellick III 5:37 pm, 8/15/2017

CHAPTER
ONE

Every day starts exactly the same for Karl Lybeck:

He wakes up at 7:32 am, his eyelids so crusted shut from allergies that he has to pry them open one lid at a time. He staggers downstairs in a sweaty pair of boxer shorts and urinates into the toilet bowl for two minutes and thirteen seconds. Then he takes a quick shower and puts on his most comfortable pair of jeans and his cleanest shirt—a navy blue polo with thin white stripes. He doesn't bother to brush his teeth. There's really no point in maintaining dental hygiene anymore.

He pours himself a bowl of Cinnamon Apple Cheerios with half a cup of recently expired milk. Karl's never been especially fond of cereal, but it's the only food he has in the house. He eats it quickly, ignoring the flavor, just trying to get something in his stomach to kill the morning hunger. Then he grabs a book from his bookshelf. It doesn't matter which one. He's read all fifty-three of them so many times that he knows each and every passage by heart. After selecting a book, he takes it outside to his backyard patio. He sits down in a slightly moist recliner while thumbing through the pages and enjoying the cool morning air.

A spider crawls three feet in his direction and then goes back the way it came. A blue jay flies past. Three grasshoppers jump in and out of his lawn, chasing each other in a dance that he has memorized well. These are Karl Lybeck's only friends, the only creatures he shares his life with now. They are as familiar to him as the eighty-seven wrinkles splitting his forever forty-year-old face.

He doesn't bother going to work today. It's been so long that he doesn't even remember exactly where he'd go. He thinks he might have been a manager in a call center. Or maybe he was a doctor, or just a high school janitor. He's not really sure. He doesn't remember much from those days. It's been a thousand lifetimes ago. At least a thousand. He's long forgotten most aspects of his life.

When the sun hits the sky, shining directly into his eyes, Karl puts down the book and goes upstairs. He digs a .35 caliber revolver out of a box hidden deep inside his closet. He doesn't remember where he got the weapon. It could have been his father's or maybe he bought it from a pawnshop on a whim. Whatever the case, Karl is thankful that he has it in his possession. It's the only thing he owns that really has any value to him anymore.

Karl polishes the metal of the gun with a fresh argyle sock and loads it with a single slug. Then he looks at himself in the mirror, presses the barrel to his temple, and pulls the trigger. There's no sound. No blast. No feeling when the bullet pierces his skull. Everything goes black.

This is his favorite part of the day. It is the part where his consciousness disappears into a blissful state of nothingness, evaporating into an eternal oblivion that seems to go on forever. It is the only time where he no longer has to think, where he no longer exists. It is more comforting than the warmest hug, more satisfying than the tastiest meal, more beautiful than any sunrise he's ever seen. But it never lasts long enough.

He always wakes up the next morning and has to do it all over again.

January awakens to her boyfriend rummaging through her purse and stealing money from her wallet.

"What the fuck are you doing?" she asks, sitting up and tossing the covers off of herself.

He turns to her and says, "Go back to sleep," as he stuffs two-hundred dollars in tens and twenties into his pocket.

When she looks him in the eyes, she doesn't recognize him. He still looks like the same Jason she always knew. He's still wearing the same clothes he was the night before when they went out to see the new King Kong movie and ate dinner at their favorite Brazilian steakhouse. But his eyes are different. It's like an older, crazier man has somehow stolen Jason's body.

"I have to go," he says. "They're coming for me."

January leaps out of bed. "What? Who's coming for you?"

"Don't worry about it." His voice is cold and foreign.

"You won't remember anything, anyway."

Then he leaves the room.

"What the hell are you talking about?" January yells, jumping out of bed and chasing him downstairs.

But Jason doesn't respond. He grabs January's car keys from the mantelpiece, goes to the front door and peeks outside to make sure the coast is clear. Then he runs for the car.

"What is wrong with you?" January grabs her shoes and goes after him, still wearing the sweatpants and tank top she slept in.

Before he can start the car, January jumps in the passenger seat and pulls the parking brake. He tries to pry her fingers off the handle, but she won't budge.

"I don't have time for this, Jan," he says. His voice is frantic, his eyes darting around her front yard like a cornered animal.

"Why are you trying to steal my fucking car?" she yells. "What is going on?"

He takes a deep breath. "I'm in trouble, okay. Just take your hand off the brake and I'll tell you on the way. We have to go."

She releases the brake and Jason slams on the gas, screeching out of the driveway at full speed.

"Are you gambling again?" she asks. "I told you I'd leave you if you didn't cut that shit out."

He lets out a nervous laugh and shakes his head. "Nothing like that."

"Then who's after you?"

"It's hard to explain…"

He pauses to focus on driving. A line of cars is stopped at a light up ahead. Jason switches lanes, speeds past them and makes a left turn. He misses an old woman crossing the road by mere inches, swerving around her as if he knew she was coming, even though it's impossible that he could've seen her.

January digs her nails into the dashboard. "Can you slow down?"

"You should have stayed home. It would have been easier."

Jason speeds up to 80 miles per hour, driving like a NASCAR driver. What baffles January the most is how good he is at driving at such a speed. He's always been such a bad driver. He doesn't even own a car because he hates driving so much, always afraid he might accidentally kill somebody. But here he is driving with such confidence that it's like he's been a professional getaway driver for over a decade.

"I'll let you out when it's safe," he says.

January shakes her head. "You still haven't explained who's after you."

Jason lets out a sigh. "Look, you're not awake yet. You wouldn't understand."

"Awake?" she asks. "I've never been more awake in my life."

He laughs and shakes his head again. "That's not what I meant." He pulls a pack of cigarettes out of January's glove compartment and lights up a smoke. January can't believe her eyes.

"You smoke now?" she asks. "How'd you even know

they were in there?"

Jason was always a strict non-smoker. He hated it so much that he insisted that she quit when they started dating. The cigarettes she kept in her glove compartment were supposed to be a secret, just in case she really needed one during a break at work. He inhales the cigarette deeply, still able to navigate through the traffic with only one hand on the wheel.

Her boyfriend doesn't explain his new smoking habit, pretending like he doesn't even have a cigarette in his hand.

Instead, he says, "I've tried to explain it to you before, but you never believe me. I'm not even going to try."

January just leans back in her seat and lets out a puff of air, completely baffled by every word that comes out of her boyfriend's mouth. It's definitely like somebody switched bodies with him. But there are a few things that still remind her of the old Jason. He still has that nervous tic in his right eye. He still has that nervous laugh. He still grunts and swears under his breath when he's stressed out. January wonders if he has always been this way and the personality she knew this whole time was all just a façade. She wonders if this is actually his true self.

As she watches him smoking a cigarette and weaving recklessly through traffic like he's playing Grand Theft Auto in real life, she realizes that she no longer wants anything to do with this man.

"I want you to pull over and let me out," January tells him. "You can take the fucking car. I don't care."

Jason looks in the rearview mirror and says, "Shit…" He tosses his cigarette out the window. "They found me." Then he slams the accelerator to the floor, increasing their speed even further.

January looks back to see a black van tailing them. It weaves through traffic just as effortlessly as Jason, quickly gaining on them.

"Who is that?"

"They're the ones who are after me," he says.

His eyes focus like an eagle's on the road. He goes through a red light, screeching around the stopped cars, narrowly missing the oncoming traffic. But it doesn't deter their pursuers. The black van gets through just as easily.

"Let me out," January cries. "You're going to get us killed."

Jason shakes his head. "I'm sorry. It's too late for that."

He turns a corner, trying to lose them, but it only helps their pursuers close the gap.

"Pull over!" January yells.

He just shakes his head at her. "I never should have gone for your wallet. You always wake up whenever I go for your wallet."

"What the fuck are you talking about?"

He doesn't answer, talking more to himself than he is to her. "You always fuck everything up when you come with me."

She grabs the parking brake and threatens to force them to stop. "If you don't stop this car I will."

"Don't!" Jason tries to shove her away from the brake, but she doesn't let go. She pulls the brake and the wheels squeal. It doesn't stop them, but it slows the car down.

The van rams them from behind and Jason loses control of the vehicle. January screams as the car spins. Jason doesn't take his foot off the gas, turning the wheel until the car is facing the opposite direction. Then he speeds forward, going back the way they came.

As they pass the van, January gets a good look at the guy in the driver's seat. The man is wearing a police officer's uniform.

"He's a cop!" she yells. "Why are you being chased by police?"

January wonders why the policeman is driving a black van instead of a police cruiser. Even if he was driving an unmarked car, she still doesn't understand why he wouldn't be flashing his lights.

"Just shut the fuck up and let me concentrate," he says. "I've never gone this way before."

Jason speeds into an intersection, through a red light, but this time he isn't as accurate as he had been before. He isn't able to weave through traffic with expert precision. He has no idea that he just drove into the path of a dump truck speeding through the green light.

January sees the truck for only a split second before it collides with the passenger side door. The car crumples. Blood splatters across Jason's face. When the car comes to a stop, January realizes the blood is hers. Her vision goes blurry. When she looks down, she sees the blood leaking into her lap. It drains like a faucet from her skull and neck. The car door is bent inward from the impact with the truck, splitting open her midsection. Her arm is bent the wrong way at the elbow, dangling between her legs. She opens her mouth to speak but nothing comes out.

Jason's eyes widen in shock. He doesn't say anything. He just unbuckles his seat belt, opens the car door and backs away. Before he can turn to run, the black van plows into him, running him over at full force.

The last thing January sees before she bleeds out is two policemen stepping out of the van, slapping handcuffs on her boyfriend and dragging his mangled body through the street. They don't realize that his brains are splattered across the asphalt.

January wakes screaming. She looks down at her body. She's no longer in her car. She's no longer bleeding or in pain. She's in her bed, under her covers. It's like none of it ever happened.

"What the fuck?" she cries, touching herself to make sure she's okay. The image of her arm bent the wrong way is still fresh in her mind.

She looks over to see Jason who is trying to sneak out of her room. His body is no longer mangled from being hit by the van. His brains are still inside his skull.

"Jason?" she asks with panic in her voice.

He groans and turns back.

"What the hell happened?" she asks. "We were hit by that truck. I was bleeding to death. You were run over…."

When Jason hears her say this, his eyes widen.

January stands up, still touching her body, searching for wounds. It couldn't possibly have been a dream. It was definitely real. But why was she back in her bed as though none of it happened?

Jason steps toward her. "You remembered that?"

She looks up at him. "You remember it, too? The car accident? Those cops in the black van that were chasing us? It wasn't a dream?"

Jason presses his eyes closed with his thumb and index finger, then shakes his head.

"Don't tell me you finally woke up…" he says.

January steps out of bed and goes to him. "What is this? What's happening? Why are we back at my place?"

Jason seems almost annoyed with her for remembering. "Why *now* of all times? Why couldn't you have woken up sooner…"

"What do you mean?"

Jason turns away from her and says, "I don't have time to explain it to you. I have to go."

He tries to leave the room but she grabs his arm.

She cries, "You can't just go. I'm freaking out here."

He pushes her away. "Things are different now. You're repeating, like me."

"Repeating?"

"I don't have time for this," he says. "You'll figure it all out eventually."

"But—"

Before January can ask him for further clarification, there's a crashing noise downstairs. Somebody has broken down her front door. Then there's a loud commotion of men yelling and stomping through her living room.

Jason panics. "Oh, fuck! They're already here!"

He runs across the room and slams the bedroom door shut, locks it, and then knocks over a bookcase to create a barricade.

"How the hell did they get here so fast?" he yells at January, even though she has far less of an idea of what's going on than he does.

"Are they the same people?" January asks.

Jason paces in a circle.

"They must've gotten new recruits…" he says. "People who live closer…" Then he kicks the fallen bookcase. "Shit!"

As the army of footsteps race upstairs, Jason runs for the window. He pulls it open and crawls outside, dangling from the window apron. Then he drops down into the bushes below.

The men outside the room kick on the door, trying to break it down, but the shelf holds it in place. January screams. She has no idea who they are or what they want. Jason pulls himself out of the bushes and takes off running.

January doesn't know what to do. As the bedroom door splits open, she decides to crawl out the window and follow him.

Without shoes, January runs through the grass to the back of her house. Jason jumps the fence into her neighbor's yard. January goes after him.

"Wait for me!" she calls out.

The sound of her voice attracts two men standing with shotguns in her front yard. They are wearing jeans and t-shirts, not police uniforms like the people who chased them yesterday.

The men yell out to the others, "They're going for the back!"

When she sees them aiming their shotguns, January screams and runs. Her feet are cut open on sharp rocks as she runs through her yard, but the adrenalin kills the pain. She doesn't realize she's bleeding until she climbs her neighbor's fence and leaves bloody footprints up the wood.

She follows her boyfriend through the neighbor's backyard, dodging a barking Rottweiler that snaps at her heels as she runs across the lawn. The two men with shotguns hop over the fence faster than January was able to with her bare feet. They don't see Jason. Just her. She knows that she's leading them right to him, but she's not sure where else to go. She's too frightened to flee in another direction.

"They're coming!" January screams at her boyfriend as he rushes toward a brick wall in the next yard.

He doesn't slow down for her. He goes as fast as he can, fleeing for his life, not giving a shit about what happens to his girlfriend.

January crawls up the brick wall, but isn't as tall or as strong as Jason. Before she gets halfway up, one of the men catches up to her and grabs her by the legs. He growls and spits as he pulls on her. He's the younger of the two men, perhaps the other one's son. He has a beard, thin-framed glasses and his hair is cut short. January can't tell if he's a redneck or a hipster.

"Stop resisting!" the man yells.

"Leave her," the other man tells him, coming up behind with the Rottweiler snapping at his heels. "We're not after the woman."

But January is in such a panic she doesn't hear them. She kicks the bearded man in the face and uses his shoulder to push herself over the wall, rolling off the top and landing in a rose bush. Her arms and legs become tangled in the branches, her skin cut open against the thorns. She's unable to escape in time.

The two men climb up the wall and hop over the bushes, leaving January behind. They raise their shotguns at Jason as he runs across the lawn.

"Stop or we'll shoot!" one of the men yells.

But Jason doesn't listen. He goes for the next wall, leaping to the ledge, struggling to pull himself up. But before he can get over, the younger of the two men opens fire and takes his head clean off.

CHAPTER
TWO

Karl Lybeck sits on his back patio, reading a copy of *James and the Giant Peach* by Roald Dahl. Even though it's a children's book, it is by far his favorite book that he owns. It's the only book out of the fifty-three that he can still enjoy after having read it over a thousand times. Every sentence is so simple, yet so perfect. His other books grew mind-numbingly boring after the first few hundred reads, but not this one. It only seems to improve with each read.

Karl flips through the book, reciting some of his favorite passages. A spider crawls three feet in his direction and then goes back the way it came. A blue jay flies past him. But he doesn't pay attention to them. He's too busy flipping through his book, smiling at the absurd cruelty of Aunt Sponge and Aunt Spiker.

He almost doesn't realize the frightened young man running through his yard until he closes his book and imagines the pictures tattooed inside of his head.

But then Karl sees another person climbing into

his backyard. A young woman, screaming and whining, kicking at somebody on the other side who has a hold of her leg. At first, Karl doesn't think it could possibly be real. He's relived this day so many times before. Nothing has ever changed. He's never seen anyone climb over the wall before.

The shock of seeing them puts him in a catatonic state. He doesn't move or say a word. He just watches as the woman rolls over the brick wall and lands in the rose bushes. His mouth widens when two men with shotguns hop over the bushes into the yard, going after another man on the other side of the lawn.

Karl thinks this must all be some kind of hallucination. He's been reliving the same day for so long that his mind must have finally snapped. He watches in disbelief as the men with shotguns race across his yard and gun down the man trying to escape over his south wall.

The young man's upper body is shredded from the buckshot; half of his face is stripped from the skull. He falls lifelessly back into the yard.

The young woman screams when she sees him die, crawling out of the bushes toward him. He must've been important to her, a brother or a boyfriend.

"What the fuck, Mickey!" an older man says to the guy who did the shooting, going over to the corpse to check for a pulse. "Our job is to take him in alive."

The man who fired rubs his beard and then shrugs. "I warned him. It's not my fault he kept running."

The older guy slaps him across the face and says, "You just got this job. Do you want to get fired on your first day?"

"What's it matter?" the bearded guy says. "It's not like I *really* killed him."

"The point is to punish him. Killing isn't a punishment anymore."

The woman staggers across the lawn, her eyes locked on the dead man. Her arms and legs are bloody. She isn't wearing any shoes.

"Why did you kill him?" she cries. "What the hell is going on?"

The two men look back at her and then look away. They aren't as guilty as they are embarrassed.

The bearded one asks, "You're not awake yet, are you?"

The older one shakes his head and says, "Jesus Christ…"

"At least she won't remember."

Their words make Karl Lybeck even more curious than their presence. They speak as if they're going through the same thing he has been going through for so many centuries. But that's impossible. He's always been the only one.

"Who are you people?" the woman asks.

"We're with the police," the older one says.

"But you're not in uniform…" she says.

"We don't have uniforms," the bearded one says.

The woman takes her eyes off of the dead man. "Are you the people who ran over him yesterday? There were these men chasing us. They drove a black van. They hit him for no reason. I think he might have died. I died, too."

The bearded man glances at her partner. "What the hell is she talking about?"

"I think she's waking up," the older man says.

Karl Lybeck clears his throat to get their attention. He's still not sure they're real, but he decides to engage them anyway. Despite gunning down a man in his yard, they haven't noticed him yet.

"Excuse me for interrupting," he says to them, "but what are you doing in my backyard?"

The three of them look over at Karl, surprised to see he was sitting there this whole time.

Karl says, "I've relived this same morning hundreds of thousands of times and this has never happened before."

The two men with shotguns look at each other and then back at him.

Karl smiles brighter than he's ever remembered smiling before.

Then he says, "It's all very exciting."

Karl Lybeck's yard is soon flooded with police officers. Only a few of them are wearing official uniforms, but they all promise they are with the police, even the ones wearing blue jeans and t-shirts and don't have the badges to prove it.

The woman is standing in her sweatpants and tank top, rubbing her arms to keep warm, facing away from her dead boyfriend that hasn't been covered or attended to in any way. The police just pretend that the corpse isn't even there.

A man in uniform with gray hair and ancient pockmarks

approaches the woman. He seems to be the only one who actually has any kind of authority, unlike the plain-clothed men with non-police-issued shotguns and hunting rifles.

"Jan Brady?" the man asks her.

"*Bradley*," she corrects him. "January Bradley."

She seems annoyed to be called a *Brady Bunch* character, as if she's suffered from this insult her entire life.

"My name's Officer Paul Pearson," he says. "They say you've only just awoken. Is this true?"

January is a wreck. She seems more upset over the confusion than her boyfriend's death.

She shakes her head. "I don't know. I don't know what's going on."

He asks, "Have you experienced an extreme case of déjà vu recently?"

She nods, wiggling her fingers nervously as she says, "Yesterday, I thought I died in a car accident. But then I woke up in my bed. The whole day started over again as if nothing happened."

"I see…" Paul Pearson pulls out a tablet from his back pocket. "What you're experiencing is completely normal. It's important to keep calm. You're not going crazy."

January takes a deep breath and then exhales, trying to calm herself.

"It's going to sound impossible," the officer says, "but for many people on this planet, the same day has been repeating itself over and over again. Today is April 17th, 2017. When you wake up tomorrow, it will be April 17th all over again. You will wake up as if none of this ever happened."

January's mind is cracking. She puts both of her hands on her head and squats in the grass. "This is bullshit. It's not happening. None of this is real…"

When Karl Lybeck hears this, he is just as shocked as January. The words Officer Paul Pearson is saying send shivers through his spine.

Karl goes to the policeman and says, "What do you mean everyone is repeating the same day over and over again? I'm not the only one?"

The policeman is confused by the man's words. He looks over at the nervous bearded man with the shotgun.

The bearded man says, "I think he's just awoken as well."

The policeman asks Karl the same thing he asked the woman. "Have you experienced an extreme case of déjà vu recently?"

Karl laughs. He says, "Yeah, you can say that."

The policeman nods. "How long have you been repeating?"

Karl shrugs. "I don't know. I've lost count."

"More than a hundred times?" Officer Pearson asks.

Karl smiles. "More than a hundred thousand."

Officer Pearson doesn't believe him. "Nobody's been repeating that long."

"I've been killing myself every morning for the last five hundred thousand days," Karl says. He doesn't know if it's actually been five hundred thousand days. He assumes it's been far more than that. "I haven't spoken to anyone during all this time. Are you saying that I wasn't the only one? All this time there were others just like me?"

The policeman ignores his question. He looks away from him. He doesn't believe a word he's saying.

"Murphy," he says to another man in uniform. "Call social services. Both of them need to go through orientation." He turns back to Karl, looks him up and down, and then looks over at January quivering in the grass. "Get them into today's newcomer class. They're going to need it."

Murphy nods at him and pulls Karl and January toward the patio, away from the other cops.

"Everything will make sense soon," Officer Pearson says to the two of them. "You're going to be fine."

But when Karl looks at January, she doesn't look like she's going to be okay for a very long time.

The policeman named Murphy brings Karl and January toward a black van parked in front of Karl's house. It's been so long since Karl has stepped out into his front yard, he'd forgotten what it looks like. He sees one of his neighbors. A bald man with a beer belly mowing his lawn. He forgets his name but he remembers being good friends with him at one point. Perhaps even best friends. It's been so many lifetimes ago that he can't be sure.

When January sees the black van, she panics. She says, "I know this van…"

Officer Murphy looks back at her. He seems annoyed with having to deal with them.

January points at the van. Then she points at Murphy. She seems to recognize him.

"It was you," she says. "You were the one driving yesterday."

Murphy just stares at her, totally disinterested.

She says, "This is the same van that chased us yesterday. This is the same van that ran over Jason."

"Just get in," Murphy says. "I've got a lot of rounds I've got to do."

"You got me killed…" January says.

Murphy shrugs. "Well, you're alive now, aren't you? Death isn't a big deal these days."

January hesitates to get into the van until the policeman pushes her inside. Karl follows after her.

"I'm taking you both to orientation," Murphy tells them as he gets into the driver's seat. "They'll explain everything to you there. It's what they do. I, on the other hand, don't give a rat's ass about how well you adjust, so keep your questions to yourself."

Even though these events have all been deeply traumatic and frightening for the woman, to Karl it is the most exciting thing that's happened to him in a very long time. He never expected that other people were in the same situation that he was. It's the first time he can remember where blowing his brains out isn't the only thing he has to look forward to.

While driving through morning traffic, Karl can't get the stupid smile off of his face. He has had absolutely nothing to get excited about for so long that he's forgotten what it's like to feel the emotion of excitement. It's exhilarating to him. Not as exhilarating as it would have been to experience a real tomorrow, but it's the next best thing. He doesn't have to be alone anymore.

Karl looks at the woman sitting next to him. She sits awkwardly in her seat, gripping her seatbelt for dear life, staring out the window as though frightened of every car that speeds by. She'd told the police she had died in a car accident the previous day. Karl assumes it's taken a toll on her psyche.

"I know how you're feeling," he tells her.

She jumps at his voice and looks over at him. It's like she'd forgotten he was sitting next to her.

He smiles. "I once killed myself by jumping off of a cliff. I used to experiment with different methods of suicide, hoping that one of them would stick. But jumping off of a cliff was the most traumatic. It takes so much longer to fall than you'd expect."

January just stares at him, not quite sure what he's talking about.

He continues, "I woke up the next morning with a deep fear of heights that I still haven't gotten over. It's crazy how scarring some experiences can be, even when death is no longer a concern."

January listens to every word he says, but doesn't

comment. She looks back at the window, watching the city pass by. Karl can tell she's seeing the world in a whole new light. He can't imagine what she's going through. He knows he must have experienced something similar when he first started repeating the same day, but it's been so long that he doesn't remember.

The woman finally breaks her silence to ask, "Is it true what you said before?" She looks over at him. "You've really been repeating the same day for that long?"

Karl nods. "It's been a very long time. I sometimes have to check my driver's license just to remember my name."

January shakes her head, unable to fathom what that would be like. "So all of this is real? We really are repeating the same day over and over again? Like in that one Bill Murray movie?"

Karl shrugs. He doesn't remember many movies, but that one is still clear in his mind. He always saw himself as the character Bill Murray portrayed, connecting with him so much that he sometimes forgets what parts of his life were his own and which were from the film.

"I guess so," Karl says. "But I always thought I was the only one. It's crazy to think others have been going through the same ordeal all this time."

"And there's no end to it?" she asks. "We'll just be doing this forever?"

Karl frowns. "I wish there was an end. But this isn't like that movie. There's nothing you can do to make time flow the way it's supposed to flow."

CHAPTER
THREE

January's stomach is twisted like a balloon animal. Her knuckles turn white from squeezing her fists into tight little balls. She can't relax for even a second during the ride across town. The memory of the car crash only gets more and more vivid as she thinks about it. A part of her can still feel what it was like to have her body crumpled inside the car. She knows that they're just phantom pains, but it doesn't make it any less real. She imagines what it would feel like to be run over by every car that she sees driving in the street.

She's relieved beyond words once they finally get to their destination. She steps out of the van and embraces the safety of the sidewalk, never wanting to enter a vehicle ever again.

"Go up to room 340," Murphy yells at them from the van. "The class starts in ten minutes. Don't be late."

Then he speeds off, leaving them by the curb.

Karl gestures toward the tall downtown office building. "Shall we go?"

January nods and heads for the entrance. Getting away from the street filled with vehicles is a comforting idea to her.

"This is going to be fun," he says as they head inside. "I can't believe this is really happening."

January doesn't know why the man is so excited about all of this. She is having a hard time grasping the reality of the situation. She feels as though she actually did die back there and all of this is just some kind of afterlife purgatory.

"I think I'm going to be sick," January says, her nerves upsetting her stomach.

"Yeah," Karl says, nodding. "I haven't even left my house in over a thousand years. Being downtown is making me dizzy as hell."

They take the elevator to the third floor and go to room 340. It's a conference room with a single table in the center. Over a dozen people are crowded around the table, waiting for the class to start. All of them look as confused and terrified as January. Only Karl enters with a giant smile on his face, sitting down right in the middle and tapping his hands against the tabletop. January sits down next to him, slouching in her chair. She tries not to close her eyes. Every time she closes them, all she sees is the accident. She tries to clear her mind until the class begins.

A woman enters the room and closes the door. She wears the suit of a business executive, black-rimmed glasses tight against her face. Her blond hair is cut into a short bob.

"Is everyone here?" she asks.

She counts all the people sitting around the table. Then she looks down at her hastily-written notes.

"Good," she says, nodding. "I'm sure you're all dying to understand what is going on, so I'll get right into it."

She clears her throat and goes to a whiteboard on the wall at the front of the table. She writes a date on the board.

"Today is April 17th 2017," she says, pointing at the date on the board. "Tomorrow will also be April 17th 2017. And every day after that will be as well."

"We already know that," says a man with short black hair and sleeve tattoos.

The woman nods. "I'm sure you all do by now, but it bears repeating. The reality of your situation has not sunken in for most of you."

"But why is it all happening?" asks an old hippy with long silver hair. "Nobody has explained that yet."

"Please hold all questions until the end," says the woman. "I promise we'll cover everything. Just be patient."

She sits down in the empty seat at the front of the table and tucks her feet neatly beneath the chair's legs.

"My name is Andrea Gray," she says. "I have been repeating this day for the equivalent of fifty-three years."

When she says this, many of the people in the conference room gasp in surprise. She just nods with sincerity.

"There are others who have been repeating it for much longer," she says. "Some have been repeating for up to five hundred years."

"But why?" asks the tattooed man, even though she explicitly said not to ask any questions.

Mrs. Gray answers him anyway, "The truth is, nobody knows exactly why. There are many speculations, but nothing concrete. The most common explanation is that we are dead and this is purgatory. I'm sure many of you have already thought this. It is the most natural way to reason with this reality, especially if you were raised with religious beliefs."

January lowers her head, almost embarrassed that she was among the people who believed she was dead.

Mrs. Gray continues, "Some people believe it was a time travel experiment that went horribly wrong. Other people believe the world was about to end and some superior alien race felt this was the only way to save humans from extinction. But why it is happening doesn't really matter. We'll likely never know for sure. It's better to just accept your new reality and focus on moving forward. You'll be happier in the long run."

"How many of us are there?" a teenage girl asks, raising her hand as if she's in just another class at school. "You know, how many people are *awake*?"

Mrs. Gray takes off her glasses and puts them on the table in front of her. She says, "As of now, at least seventy percent of the population is *awake*."

The room quiets down, trying to process that information. The only one who seems excited by this idea is Karl

Lybeck, who bounces in his seat with excitement.

"*Awake* is the term we use to describe those who have become aware that they're stuck in the time loop," says Mrs. Gray. "Every day, hundreds of new people *wake up* and begin repeating, just as you have now. We believe that it's only a matter of time before everyone on the planet joins us."

"That many?" January asks. "Are you serious?"

Mrs. Gray nods. "It's mostly children who haven't been repeating. Only about ten percent of people under the age of thirteen are awake. We don't know why exactly. Perhaps it's because their brains aren't as developed. Or perhaps if there is an intelligence behind the time loop they decided to have pity on our young." She looks across the table and asks, "Do any of you have young children?"

Four of the people in the room raise their hands.

"As far as you know, are any of them awake?" she asks.

All four of them lower their hands.

"Count yourselves lucky," she says. "It's easier to adapt without having to worry about your children being awake. It is believed that children have a harder time adjusting than adults. Knowing that they'll never be able to grow up and become an adult is a hard thing for children to accept." She lowers her head. "It will be hard for you as parents as well."

Mrs. Gray organizes her notes, scanning through them as though looking for where to go next. She pauses on one page, reads through it, and then puts it back down.

She looks up at the group and says, "This new reality will be very difficult for some of you. It comes with its share of challenges and advantages. For instance, those of you who are in a good place in your life will have an easier time of it. If you live in a nice house, or even a clean house, you'll be better off than someone who is poor or in a bad living situation."

The man with the sleeve tattoos raises his hand. Mrs. Gray ignores him at first, but he's persistent. She reluctantly calls on him.

"I don't actually live here," he says. "I'm from Boston. I was on tour with my band. Does that mean I'm always going to wake up in the back of our tour bus every morning? Forever?"

Mrs. Gray sighs and then nods at him. "I'm sorry, but yes. It's something you're going to have to deal with."

"But none of my bandmates are awake yet," he says. "They thought I was crazy when I tried to explain what was happening to me."

Mrs. Gray says, "We have counseling sessions for those of you that are in difficult situations like this. After the class, come see me if you'd like to sign up for one."

She cuts the man off before he's able to say anything else. She stands up and paces around the table.

"There are many positives and negatives of repeating," she says. "I recommend you focus on the positives. For instance, if you're a smoker you'll never have to worry about getting cancer. You can have unprotected sex without worrying about sexually transmitted diseases or pregnancy."

Many people giggle when she says this, but she says it with a straight face, as though she's said it so many times that it doesn't faze her in the slightest.

"You no longer have to pay rent or worry about being evicted," she says. "You'll never get a hangover no matter how much you drink. You'll never gain weight no matter how much you eat. You never have to worry about global warming or nuclear war or natural disasters or going hungry. You will never grow old. You will never get sick. You will never die."

"We never have to go to work!" somebody yells with excitement.

Everyone claps and cheers at that comment, but Mrs. Gray shakes her head at them.

"Unfortunately, you still have to go to work," she says. "You will still need money."

The cheers turn into moans and the excitement in the room dies.

Mrs. Gray explains, "When I first woke up, things were much different than they are now. Everything was chaos. People did what they wanted. Took what they wanted. Nobody went to work. Nobody did much of anything but drink and steal and fuck and kill each other."

A few people applaud that idea, but she glares at them until they quiet down.

"But we brought civilization back from the chaos," she says. "We created laws and punishment for breaking those laws. The time loop has completely changed how our society works. We now live exclusively by our memories. You will still need to go to work in order to earn money because your bank account will change by the time you wake up tomorrow. There are people who have your financial information memorized when they go to sleep each night and update your bank account before you wake up in the morning. This was done so that everyone would still have a reason to work. Otherwise, society would shut down. No stores or restaurants would be open. Nobody would be running the city. It would be like the post-apocalypse each and every day. And, believe me, it's not a world you want to live in. I had to go through it for years. It is the reason I now dedicate my life to helping newcomers like you."

She takes off her suit coat, revealing sweat stains under her arms. She looks at each of them directly in the eyes.

Her tone becomes more severe as she says, "I want you all to understand the importance of keeping order in our society. I need you to understand that even though your life resets at the end of each day, there are still consequences to your actions."

January looks over at Karl. The smile has finally faded from his face. Mrs. Gray stares directly at her until she looks away from Karl.

As though speaking specifically to January, she says, "And if you break the law, the punishment will be severe."

After being lectured for nearly an hour, Mrs. Gray lets them out for a fifteen-minute break. There is a table out in the hall with orange juice, coffee, and doughnuts. Everyone is quiet, their hands shaking as they fill paper cups with coffee. January couldn't even pay attention to half of what Mrs. Gray was saying in there. The woman told them about all the laws, about how murder and theft and assault are still serious crimes even though they don't mean the same thing anymore. But as hard as she tried, January couldn't pay attention. She's still in shock over everything that's happened.

"This is some bullshit," says the hippy guy with long silver hair. "I'm going to be stuck in the same dead-end job forever? Just pumping gas each and every day for eternity?"

A woman with short black hair and horn-rimmed glasses says, "She didn't say that. She just said you have to keep working."

"Yeah, but how the hell am I going to get a new job?" the hippy asks. "I didn't go to college. I don't have any experience."

The short-haired woman says, "You've got all the time in the world. You can learn new skills. Go to the library. Read books. Now that time is endless, we have the opportunity to learn how to do pretty much everything imaginable."

The woman smiles at this idea. She seems excited by the prospect. Others start to ease up, realizing that maybe the time loop could be a blessing instead of a curse.

But Karl ruins it for them by saying, "It doesn't work like that."

The whole group turns to him. He stuffs doughnut after doughnut into his mouth, relishing the flavor as though he hasn't eaten one in over a thousand years.

They wait for him to gulp down the chunks of dough in his mouth. Then he says, "Your memory isn't infinite. You'll forget more than you'll learn."

The short-haired woman shakes her head. "I've got a great memory. I plan to use it."

Karl just smiles and shakes his head. "How much do you remember from what you learned back in school?"

"I don't know," she says. "Quite a bit."

"Fifty percent?" he asks. "Thirty percent? Ten?"

"At least fifty," she says.

"And when were you last in school?" he asks.

"Eight years ago."

"Do you think you remembered more than fifty percent the year after you graduated?"

She nods. "Yeah, I probably remembered ninety percent of it. Maybe a hundred."

He says, "Well, if what you remembered decreased by forty percent after eight years, imagine how much you'll forget after a hundred years? Or a hundred thousand? It will all be completely lost."

She shakes her head. "I'm not going to forget."

"I was just like you when I first started repeating," Karl says. "I learned twelve languages. I learned how to take apart car engines and put them back together. I even learned law and medicine. But I forgot all of it. You will forget everything eventually, as well."

The hippy guy squints his eyes at Karl. "How the fuck do you know?"

January says, "He's been awake for a very long time. Even longer than Mrs. Gray."

The short-haired girl says, "Then why is he in orientation with us?"

"Until this morning, I thought I was the only one," Karl says. "But I've been going through this for a very long time. I promise you, you'll forget everything you ever knew. I don't even remember my family or childhood. Memory is far more limited than you'd think."

The group goes quiet, lowering deeper into depression. January wonders if maybe Karl should have kept that bit of information to himself. It's not something they needed to know on their first day.

"Actually, that's not entirely true," says Mrs. Gray from the doorway.

They all turn to her.

"Come back inside and I'll explain," she says.

"Memory is a muscle," she tells them. "If you exercise your memory it will become stronger. So from now on, you will want to do memory exercises each and every day. Physical exercise means nothing now. You'll never be able to get into better physical shape than you are now. But your brain can still improve. You just have to work at it. There's no reason why you can't learn new skills, learn *all* skills, as long as you keep up with your mental exercises." She holds up the papers in her hand. "I write everything down in order to remember. All the information I want to keep in my head I write down over and over again. By the time I wake up, the words will have disappeared from the pages but the practice keeps the information in my brain."

Karl snickers to himself, interrupting Mrs. Gray. Everyone looks at him.

"You have something to add, Mr. Lybeck?" she asks.

He shrugs. "No matter how many exercises you do, it's still not enough. You can wake up and do nothing but memory exercises for years, but you'll still forget plenty. So much information will slip through the cracks that you'll eventually give up."

The instructor glares at Karl, annoyed by his argument.

"What would you know?" she asks. "There are people who have more knowledge memorized than any human ever thought possible and they have been repeating for over five hundred years."

Karl snickers again. "Well, I've been repeating for over five thousand years and I tell you that it's a useless practice. You'll forget it all eventually."

Mrs. Gray sneers and shakes her head. "You've been repeating for five thousand years? That's impossible. Nobody's been repeating that long."

Karl shrugs. "Well, I have."

"How?" she asks. "Why are you even here if you've been repeating that long?"

"Because when I started repeating, I was the only one," Karl says. "I didn't know anyone else was the same as me until this morning."

Mrs. Gray shakes her head, unable to believe his words. It's like she thinks he's just messing with her or maybe he is crazy and actually believes what he's saying. Either way, she dismisses his words and continues.

"The whole world works on memory now," she says. "You'll have to get used to that. Those who don't focus on exercising their memory are the ones who have the hardest time making it in this new world, so I recommend you do everything you can to prevent letting your memory go flabby and weak. There are janitors who have become CEOs of profitable companies because they strengthened their memories over dozens of years. Some of our most brilliant minds are mere teenagers who never had a job in their lives. The possibilities are endless for you. You just need to work hard and never give up."

But no matter what she says, Karl just shakes his head and laughs like he's listening to a seven-year-old child with aspirations to become the president of the world.

They spend all day in the conference room. Everyone is so burned out and exhausted from this information that they can barely stay awake.

"The last thing I want to discuss is your sleeping practices," says Mrs. Gray. "It is important to go to sleep at a reasonable time each night. The day does not reset for you until after you go to sleep, no matter what time that is."

The man with the sleeve tattoos asks, "What happens if you don't go to sleep? I'm not a good sleeper. I've been able to stay awake for days at a time."

Mrs. Gray nods. "This is the most problematic part of our new society. It is possible to stay awake until April 18th or April 19th or even later than that. This is what we call the *neverday*. It is a false tomorrow. Anything that happens during this time will not be remembered by anyone, not even those who are awake. It is our most forbidden law to stay awake for longer than twenty-four hours after you wake up. Those who are caught breaking this law are punished most severely. And believe me, we'll know if you do. Even though nobody will remember anything that you do during the neverday, we have methods for catching people who go there. So just don't do it. We have a saying now: *don't stay awake too long*. We say it instead of goodbye or goodnight. There's nothing good that will come from staying awake. I know how it feels to long for tomorrow, but you won't get to tomorrow in the neverday. It's better if you forget it even exists."

When the class is finally wrapped up, January turns to Karl and asks, "Do you know what she's talking about with the neverday?"

Karl shrugs, "I guess. I've tried to stay awake into the next day before, but I always fall asleep eventually. There never seemed to be much of a point. No matter when I'd go to sleep, I'd always wake up at the same time. Everything would always reset. I thought about trying to stay awake forever, so that my days would actually progress, but I never had much success. I pass out pretty easily when I'm tired."

They stand up to leave, following the others out of the room.

"But why is it so bad to stay awake that long? What's wrong with it?"

Karl shrugs. "Well, I guess you could do anything you wanted and nobody would remember. Any money you spent wouldn't be taken out of your bank account. It messes with their laws of society. They seem pretty adamant about keeping everyone under control so that everything doesn't spiral into chaos."

"But doesn't it seem weird to you?" she asks.

Karl shrugs again.

Before they leave the room, Mrs. Gray stops them.

"Miss Bradley? Mr. Lybeck?" she calls out.

They turn around.

She holds up two pieces of paper that were faxed to her before the class. "After reading over your files, I think you both should sign up for counseling sessions. We have groups that meet here every day. I think it would help you."

January looks at her and back at Karl. She shakes her head. "I don't think I'm interested in any of that. I think I just need some time alone for a while."

Mrs. Gray doesn't let her off the hook.

"You were killed in a car accident on your first rotation," she says. "That's going to leave a mark that you won't easily get over. Not to mention the severity of your boyfriend's crimes and your involvement with him. You're lucky you weren't charged with aiding and abetting. This isn't a request. You are obligated by law to take part in these sessions."

January sighs and says, "Fine. Whatever."

Mrs. Gray turns to Karl. "And the fact that you say you've been repeating for thousands of years is an issue. Either you're delusional or you actually have been awake for that long. Whatever the truth, you should be attending a therapy group. You aren't obligated, but I strongly advise it."

Karl smiles and nods. "Sure, I'd love to. Any new experience is worthwhile to me."

"Very good," Mrs. Gray says. "I'll sign you both up. Be here by 9 am tomorrow. You won't have to go to work during these sessions and your bank accounts won't be updated. Just don't be late."

Karl nods and they leave the room.

"What kind of bullshit is that?" January asks.

"It should be fun," Karl says. "I can't even remember the last time I've had this much fun."

But January has no idea what's so enjoyable about all of this. It feels like she just went through orientation explaining what life will be like on her first day in hell.

CHAPTER
FOUR

The next day, Karl wakes up with a newfound enthusiasm for life. He takes a longer shower than usual. He actually brushes his teeth and uses deodorant. He puts on his nicest clothes, rather than his most comfortable. And for breakfast, he goes to the corner shop for a microwave burrito. He pays with three of the seven dollars he has in his wallet. It's the only money that he ever has to spend on anything.

Karl meets January at the bus stop in their neighborhood, licking vinegary hot sauce from his fingers.

"Not driving?" Karl asks.

She looks at him from the bench and shakes her head. She doesn't need to explain why.

"Me neither, he says. "I don't even remember how."

She just nods. Even the act of taking the bus seems to have her on edge.

"How'd it go with your boyfriend this morning?" Karl asks. "Did the cops come for him again?"

She shrugs. "He was gone when I woke up."

Karl nods and sits down next to her.

"That's probably for the best," Karl says. "You don't want to have to deal with the cops. They seem like assholes these days."

"Cops were always assholes," January says.

"They were?" Karl asks. "I don't really remember."

"They still came to my house this morning," she says. "They said they want me to come by the station after our session today."

"What do they want?"

She shrugs. "I think they want to ask me questions about Jason. I'm not sure."

"Sounds like a pain."

January nods at him.

"All of this is a pain," she says.

They take the bus downtown, back to the same building of their orientation. When they arrive in the lobby, they are told to take the elevator up to the eighteenth floor, to Room 1803.

The room is being taken apart when they arrive. A group of about seven people is in there, pushing desks against the walls and placing chairs in a circle in the center of the room.

"Is this the group session?" January asks them.

A man in a sweater vest looks up and smiles. "Are you the new people?"

He goes to them and introduces himself. "I'm Nick. I run the sessions. You've both just woken, right?"

Karl notices tags on his clothes, like he just purchased them on the way over. He wonders if the man has to purchase these clothes every day before work, perhaps because he has nothing else clean in the house and it's faster than doing laundry, or perhaps he didn't own anything appropriate when his rotation began.

"Sort of," Karl says. "We just did orientation yesterday."

Nick nods and shakes his hand.

"Very good," he says. His smile looks fake, like he's had it plastered on his face day in and day out for so long that he doesn't even realize it's there.

"Help us set up," he says. "We'll be starting any minute now."

The two newcomers agree, but there's not much for them to do. The room's basically already set up for the session.

Karl wonders what the space was originally used for. There aren't any personal belongings on any of the desks, so it must have been a business that recently closed shop just before the day started repeating. These people must have repurposed it for helping those who have freshly awoken in town. It amazes Karl how well they've adapted to repeating. Because he was alone, he didn't have the opportunity to create anything out of his life. He's kind of envious of the people who were able to create this new society while he was staying home and killing himself. He kind of regrets giving up on life all those thousands of rotations ago.

When they're ready to begin, January and Karl take their seats. They sit as far away from Nick as possible. January pushes her chair a couple of feet back before she sits in order to separate herself from the circle, even if it's just by the slightest bit. Karl sits next to her but keeps the seat where it is.

The room fills before Nick begins. There are about fifteen other people in the circle of chairs. Unlike the group from yesterday, these people don't seem nervous and scared. They look depressed and worn out. The endless cycle of repetition has taken its toll on the lot of them. They've most likely been awake for a much longer amount of time than January.

"Welcome, everyone," Nick says, his fake smile still plastered across his face as he speaks. "I trust everyone has had a pleasant morning?"

Another person barges into the room. It's the guy with the sleeve tattoos Karl saw at orientation the day before.

"Is this the right place?" the young man asks.

Nick looks down at his notebook and asks, "Are you… Mitch Murphy?"

The tattooed man nods. "Yeah. I don't wake up until nine."

"It's okay," Nick says. "Please, take a seat."

When Mitch sees Karl and January, he goes right for them, as though seeking safety in familiar faces, even though they didn't speak a word to each other the day before. He sits next to Karl and groans, taking off a patch-covered backpack and dropping it to his feet. The smell of tobacco smoke drifts off of his leather jacket and assaults the people next to him. Karl hasn't smelled cigarette smoke for so long that it's almost pleasant to him. It makes him consider picking up smoking again.

"So we've got three new people today," Nick says, looking directly at Karl. "Do any of you wish to begin?"

Mitch, January and Karl look at each other, but none of them want to be the first to start.

"I just got here," Mitch says, shaking his head.

Nick smiles and nods. "Don't worry about it. There's no pressure." He looks to his right, glancing over at a large bald man with a belly bulging beneath his tight white t-shirt. "Tony, why don't you start?"

The bald man shrugs. "Yeah, sure."

But he just sits there, staring down at the floor and rubbing his neck. Karl realizes that he's also got a split lip and a black eye.

"Whenever you're ready," Nick says.

The man takes another minute before he begins. He rubs his greasy scalp and coughs thick phlegm from his throat and then swallows it.

"Yeah, so I'm Tony," he says. "I've been awake for about two hundred days now."

Nick nods at him to continue.

"Yeah, so it's been a living hell for me," Tony says. "The day before the repetition I lost my job and my girlfriend left me. I don't care about any of that, but I did what any guy would do after having an exceptionally bad day. I got trashed. I downed a six pack of beer and a bottle of cheap whiskey, and that's before I even hit the bar. I don't remember much of what happened after that. I know I drank my whole paycheck away, because my bank account was empty." He points at his black eye. "I also must've gotten into a fight. I don't know who it was, but they must have kicked my ass pretty bad. It still hurts like a motherfucker. And it always will."

He pauses to cough up more phlegm and rubs his head.

"So, yeah, I woke up with the worst fucking hangover of my life," he says. "And I've been waking up with that hangover every day since." He puts his face in his hands and shakes his head. "They say I'll get used to it eventually but it's not gotten any better. Every day, it seems to only get worse."

Karl cringes at the thought of being trapped in an endless hangover. He knows how bad it is to repeat the same day over and over again, but at least he wasn't sick or hungover. Since it's April, he has bad allergies he's had to deal with, but allergies are nothing compared to what this man has had to endure.

"I've tried everything to get over my hangover," Tony continues. "People have said to try taking long walks, going for a swim, taking cold showers, downing energy drinks filled with vitamin B. But the only thing that really works is drinking it off. I've experimented with it many times over. Three glasses of top-shelf vodka kills the hangover and gives me a good buzz for a few hours. But now I have to decide between being horribly sick and being an alcoholic. I long for feeling what it's like to be sober again. I just want to be normal."

"Have you tried the pills yet?" Nick asks.

Tony shakes his head. "They're too damned hard to find."

"I've been told they work wonders," Nick says. "They might not clear your hangover completely, but people in your condition have said they're lifesavers."

Tony says, "Yeah, and so many people need them now that they've raised the price through the roof. And there's only so many in supply."

"Have you tried cocaine?" Mitch asks him.

Tony looks at the newcomer, interested in what he has to say.

"Cocaine will cure a hangover better than anything you can buy over the counter," Mitch says.

"Seriously?" Tony asks, a smile creeping on his face.

"We've got some in my tour bus," Mitch says. "I can hook you up."

Tony leans in closer. "That would be amazing, man. Does it really work?"

Nick holds up his hands to intervene. "Hey, guys. Cocaine is still illegal. If you continue I'll have to report this."

The bald man sneers. "Fuck you, Nick. I'll do anything if it will help me out."

Mitch adds, "Why is cocaine even illegal anymore? It's not like it's going to do any damage. Even if you overdose, it's not going to kill you."

"We have to stick to the laws," Nick says. "Without laws, there's chaos. Perhaps they'll legalize it someday, but until then you can't do it." He turns to Mitch. "And you should flush the cocaine you have every morning before you're caught with it. Otherwise, the consequences are severe."

Mitch shrugs. "It's not mine. It's the drummer's shit. And he's not awake yet. The dude will kick my ass if I try to flush it."

Nick just shakes his head and tries to change the subject.

"Let's have somebody else talk for now," he says, looking around the room. He points at a black woman a few seats away from Karl. "Sheri, why don't you go?"

The woman nods.

But before she begins, Mitch and Tony look at each other, exchanging nods like they plan to meet up after the session is out.

"My name's Sheri," the woman says. "I've been repeating for almost fifty days."

Karl looks over at her. She wears sweatpants and a baggy t-shirt. She seems a bit overweight with a chubby face, but was probably beautiful at one time. She's not wearing any makeup. If Karl had to guess, he'd say she's in her late twenties or early thirties.

"So my problem is pretty obvious," she says, holding out her stomach. Karl notices the massive bulge to her belly. "I'm nine months pregnant. I was supposed to be due any day now. But that day's never going to come. If any of you have had kids you know the hell of being pregnant. It's all worth it once the baby's born, but..."

She pauses to collect herself, as though trying not to cry.

"But this baby's never coming out," she says with a laugh, even though her eyes are beginning to water.

She takes a long pause to wipe her eyes.

"Don't worry, Sheri," Nick says. "Take your time."

When she's ready to continue, Sheri says, "I can deal with the pain and discomfort. But the idea that my baby's never going to be born... The fact that I'll never get to hold her in my arms... That I'll never get to know who she is... That's what's hard. That's what I can't get over."

She breaks out into tears, unable to hold them back. Outside of Karl and January, the group seems unmoved by her words. They've probably heard it a dozen times before. Or perhaps they don't care because they're suffering from issues just as bad, or worse, than hers.

"Part of me wonders if it's better this way," she says. "If she was born and stayed a baby forever, that might be harder." Then she looks down and smiles. "It might be cute to always have a baby around. At least I'd know what she looks like."

"It's not fun," an Indian woman interjects. "I have three young ones at home. One is just a baby. None of them are awake yet. It's a living nightmare."

Nick hushes her down. "Riya, it's not your turn. Let Sheri speak."

The black woman continues, "I'm also dealing with

very little sleep. I haven't been able to sleep well in my condition. The night before I began repeating, I only had maybe an hour of sleep. So I'm constantly tired. If I ever take a nap, I just wake up at the beginning of the day all over again. I don't even remember what it feels like to have a good night's sleep."

Karl is kind of envious of her. If he was tired enough to go back to sleep, he wouldn't have had to kill himself every morning.

"Have you tried meditation like I recommended?" Nick asks.

She nods. "Yeah, it helps. I've also found that sleeping lightly is even better. As long as I don't fall into a deep sleep, the day doesn't restart. It's the only thing that gets me through each day. But it's difficult. I pass out way too easily. I have to set my alarm for fifteen minutes at a time or else I'm gone."

Nick nods at her. "Very good. I'm glad that's working out for you."

The woman shrugs at him. It seems like cat naps and meditation aren't enough. When Karl looks over at Mitch, he wonders if the guy is thinking about offering her some cocaine as well.

The next person to speak is a middle-aged white guy who shaves his head so that it doesn't look like he's balding. But because the hair has grown back a little, the bald spot and receding hairline are clear to everyone.

"My name's Lyle Conway," he says. "I've been repeating for only fourteen days."

Nick says, "You've never spoken here yet, have you?"

Lyle shakes his head. "I don't really like to talk in front of people. I'm kind of uncomfortable in these kinds of situations, I guess."

Nick nods at him. "Most people are. Don't worry about it. Nobody's judging you."

Lyle shrugs. "I feel stupid talking about it. All of your problems seem so much worse than mine."

"That's okay," Nick says. "This isn't a competition. A problem that seems small to others could be a big deal to somebody else. Either way, it helps to talk about it."

Lyle nods his head and says, "Well, my problem is a lack of fulfillment, I guess. My whole life I've been a writer. I wrote crime novels. It's the only job I've ever had since my twenties."

He pauses, getting nervous. Most writers have problems with social awkwardness. Even if they didn't start out that way, working by yourself and rarely leaving the house will do that to you.

"Now that the day is repeating, I have no idea what to do with myself," Lyle says. "I can't finish the book I've been working on for the past five months. Every time I go to sleep, the words I write disappear. It's frustrating as hell. The only books I'll ever write are the ones that are already finished. Anything I do from now on won't last. I'll never be able to finish another book, no matter how long I live in this endless cycle."

Nick tries to hide it, but doesn't seem to pity him one bit, not any more than the other people in the room.

"Many creative types have passed through here with this same problem," he says. "But just because the day is repeating, that doesn't mean that you can't still succeed as a writer."

Lyle is confused by his statement. He doesn't believe him. He smirks and says, "How's that?"

Nick explains himself, "Well, before printed books we had an oral tradition. Stories were passed down by telling them to others. Around a campfire. In front of an audience. You can still tell stories for a living. I know writers in town who do live readings of stories they've memorized in their heads. They charge for tickets. You can still use your skills, even in the new world."

Lyle shrugs. "But who would pay for that? There are plenty of books out there that they could read. Personally, I wouldn't go to a reading when I've got a library full of books."

Nick shakes his head. "You'd be surprised. There are many people who have been repeating for so long that they've read all the books in the library. They've watched all the movies they could find. They're all dying for new stories. You could fill that niche."

"And people are actually doing this already?" Lyle asks.

"There are a few writers in town who have been successful with live storytelling," Nick says. "You should get to know them."

Lyle nods but doesn't seem enthusiastic about the idea.

"You can also write online," Nick says. "There are

authors who charge for online subscriptions to their books. They post one chapter a day, as they write it. Even though it disappears by the morning, people are able to keep up with the story until it's finished. Major writers are able to charge up to a thousand dollars per reader per book they write. You can still make a living this way."

Lyle seems offended by this idea. "But that goes against the whole purpose of writing. You don't have a book that you can hold in your hands. You don't have a story that lives on forever. Nobody can read your back catalog. It sounds horrible."

"At least you're not an artist like me," says a black man with long dreadlocks.

Everyone turns to him.

The guy with dreadlocks smirks at the writer and says, "My skills are useless now that I'm repeating. The business of art is convincing people that your work will be of value after you die. But nobody buys art anymore. The only way I can make a living is by selling art on street corners to people who haven't woken up yet. It's a bitch and a half. I *wish* I could be a writer and charge people to see my work online."

Lyle quiets down. He must know his problems aren't as bad as the others in the room, even when it comes to other creative types.

But then he says, "How can their books even be any good writing like that? It takes me months slaving over every single word. I'm a perfectionist. I can't imagine writing a whole chapter a day. I wouldn't have time for revisions. It would be terrible. And knowing that no matter how much work I put into it the words would disappear at the end of the day? How could I possibly deal with that?"

Nick shrugs at him. "When the world gives you lemons, you don't wish for strawberries. You make lemonade and move on. A writer who goes blind or loses his hands has to deal with his limitations and figure out a way to keep working. You have to figure this out for yourself. Perhaps there's another passion of yours that you have yet to explore. You have all the time in the world. You can figure it out."

Lyle groans at him. He says, "Writing is all I've ever done. It's all I care to do. I'd rather die than give it up. If I actually could die, that's exactly what I'd do."

Nobody else in the room seems to have any pity for him. The artist with dreadlocks snorts and lets out a quick chuckle, as though he's saying *pussy* under his breath. The pregnant woman rolls her eyes.

"You've got plenty of time to figure it out," Nick says. "Maybe you'll find a new way to use your art or maybe you'll discover something else in life that you're passionate about. Even though we live in a different world with a new set of hurdles to overcome, creativity is still a very useful commodity. The world is still your oyster."

Nick's fake smile glows so brightly that it only pisses off the man it's directed toward.

Lyle opens his mouth as if to argue with all his passion at the leader of the group.

But before he's able to speak, Tony says, "At least you're not forever hungover like I am."

And that shuts the writer right up.

"Okay…" Nick says. "Now that a few regulars have gone, why don't we hear from one of the newcomers."

He looks at Mitch, Karl, and January.

January says, "I'd prefer not to today."

The tone of her voice is so stern that Nick doesn't bother questioning it. He turns to Mitch, but the young punk doesn't look him in the eye. He digs through his backpack, pretending to be busy. So Nick turns to the last of them, Karl, who doesn't have any good excuse not to go next.

"How about you?" Nick asks.

Karl shrugs. "Yeah, sure."

"Excellent." Nick smiles. "Begin when you're ready."

Karl nods his head and begins right away.

"My name is Karl Lybeck," he says. "I've been repeating for so long that I have no idea exactly how long it has been."

Nick says, "A rough estimate would be fine."

Karl says, "I don't know how many days, but it's probably been the equivalent of fifty thousand years. Probably much more than that."

Everyone looks at him with confused faces. Nick giggles, assuming he's just making a joke of it.

"Seriously, how long have you been awake?" Nick asks.

"I'm not joking," Karl says. "When I started repeating,

I was the only one. There wasn't anyone else, at least nobody I met. Definitely nobody in this city. I thought I was the only one."

Nick doesn't giggle after Karl says this. He realizes that he might be telling the truth, or at least thinks he's telling the truth.

"But how is that possible?" Nick asks. "Nobody has been repeating for that long. The man who has been awake the longest is Michael Stockman. He's been repeating for the equivalent of seven hundred years. Nobody has been doing this for over a thousand, let alone fifty thousand."

"Well, I have," he says.

"I'm finding it hard to believe," Nick says.

Karl stares him down. "Are you going to let me speak or keep interrupting me?"

Nick smiles and nods his head. "I'm sorry. Please continue."

Karl starts over. "My name's Karl Lybeck and I've been repeating for so long that I don't really remember much of my old life at all. For as long as I remember, I've been killing myself soon after waking up in order to cope with my immortality. I've done pretty much everything you can imagine in our situation, but eventually everything lost its appeal. The only thing I wished for was a permanent death.

"I'm sure many of you see repeating as a living hell. I wasn't hungover or pregnant or had a career I cared about. But even as a normal person with a decent life, repeating for as long as I have is an unending state of torment. I wished for so long for something to change.

Anything. But it was all just endless repetition.

"The only reason I didn't kill myself today is because I've learned that there's many more people who are repeating. I'm excited for this new society that's been built. It's given me a reason not to kill myself every morning."

When Karl finishes, a large smile stretches across his face. But everyone just stares at him. They don't seem to know what to make of him. He realizes his words might seem farfetched, but he told them nothing but the truth.

"But I still don't know if this is true…" Nick says, his fake smile finally leaving his face. "How could you possibly be repeating for so long without meeting anyone else? There was a time when there was nothing but chaos. People were killing each other in the streets. There were explosions. The whole city has been set on fire. I've been awake for the equivalent of 100 years and I couldn't imagine thinking I was the only one even if I killed myself every day."

Karl shrugs. "I don't know. Nothing's ever changed for me. I never noticed any explosions or fires. Perhaps I killed myself before they happened. Or perhaps they just didn't happen on my side of town. I'm not lying, though. You don't have to believe me, but this is the truth."

Nick shakes his head. "But it's so farfetched…"

Karl doesn't respond. It's not like he's going to lie to make the man more comfortable with his idea of reality. He's lived so long that he doesn't really care what anyone else thinks.

Nick changes his tone, realizing he's being too judgmental and closed-minded.

"For the sake of fairness, I'll believe you," Nick says. "Whether it's true or not doesn't matter. What I'm most worried about is how you've dealt with your problems. Suicide is never the answer, even in this world. It is actually a very common problem among people who have come through here. But, trust me, killing yourself isn't good for you. You can find a place in society without giving up."

Karl notices January covering her mouth and trying not let on that she's giggling after Nick said *killing yourself isn't good for you*. She seems to be the only one who sees the absurdity in that comment.

"Oh, I don't plan on killing myself anymore," Karl says. "Now that things are different, I'm excited to be a part of this new world. If it turns out to be boring I can always start killing myself again, maybe a few hundred years from now."

Nick shakes his head. "No, you shouldn't kill yourself ever again, no matter how boring and repetitive things get. What would happen if everyone just killed themselves after waking up? What kind of world would that be? We can't have that. Society depends on each and every one of us taking an active role in keeping it going. I can't stress the importance of this enough."

Karl shrugs. "As I said, you have nothing to worry about with me. I'm not going to go back to killing myself."

"Are you sure?" Nick asks. "If not there's a group for suicide addicts that you might want to join."

January giggles even louder behind her hand. She's not able to hold back anymore. Everyone turns to her.

"Is there a problem, Miss Bradley?" Nick asks.

67

She shakes her head and says, "I'm sorry. It's nothing."

But Nick won't let it go. He keeps staring with his stupid smile until she explains herself.

"It's just that…" she says. "Is there really a group for suicide addicts? That's actually a thing?"

Nick's smile leaves his face. "It's nothing to laugh about. Suicide is a serious problem in our world now. There are people like Mr. Lybeck here, who use suicide to escape the monotony. There are people who kill themselves because they have problems like Tony, where they're too sick or hungover or in too much pain to face each day. Depression is very common. There are also people who kill themselves just for the experience. It's like a drug to them. There's even some who see killing themselves as a sexual fetish. I know a man who pays women to choke him to death. There's another man who is turned on by being stabbed. And a woman who likes to have her blood sucked out of her neck by men or other women pretending to be vampires."

January laughs out loud when she hears this. She doesn't even try to hide it. Everyone but Karl gives her a dirty look.

"I'm sorry," she says. "All of this has just been too crazy for me. It's all so ridiculous. I feel like I'm going crazy."

Nick nods his head. "Would you like to go next? I'd like to hear about your experience."

January says, "Not today. I'm not ready."

"Are you sure?" Nick asks.

She nods.

"I'm sorry for interrupting," she says.

Nick lets her slide this time. "As long as we hear from you tomorrow, I'll give you a pass."

She agrees.

Nick looks around the room for somebody to call on next, but nobody else seems willing to speak. Everyone's exhausted and depressed. They all seem like they're counting the minutes until they can finally go home. Everyone except for Karl, who kind of wants to keep speaking. His talk was cut short. He had many more things he wanted to say. But he decides to sit back and listen. He knows that he has all the time in the world to speak to people who will actually, finally, remember what he tells them.

CHAPTER
FIVE

When the session is over, January says a quick goodbye to Karl and takes the bus across town to the police station, where she was asked to go by the young bearded man who showed up at her doorstep that morning, brandishing his non-police-issue shotgun. The same man who murdered her boyfriend the previous day.

She is greeted by Officer Paul Pearson in the lobby, surrounded by a group of new recruits—men in plain clothes, carrying weapons they brought from home that range from revolvers to hunting rifles to even a submachine gun. It's like he's an old west sheriff gathering together a posse in order to hunt down an outlaw gang. But these deputies don't seem to be the brightest men to trust in positions of authority. Half of them don't even seem to speak English and look like day workers he picked up outside of a Home Depot. They seem more likely to shoot themselves in the foot than take down a criminal. The other half look a little too excited to be there, like they only came because they want to shoot people without going to jail for it.

"They outnumber us ten to one," Pearson says to the group. "You have to be fast and efficient. Don't be sloppy. I have enough morons on staff already. I don't need any more."

As January walks across the lobby, Pearson sees her on the other side of the posse and gives her a nod, using his eyes to tell her that he'll just be a moment.

"Wake up bright and early and do your job," he says. "Practice getting out of your house as fast as you can. Every second counts."

Then he waves them away, patting their backs as they disperse. He doesn't let them past the reception area of the station, like they don't have clearance as new recruits. They fill their cups with coffee before they go.

"Jan Brady?" Pearson asks her.

She sneers at him. "*Bradley.* January Bradley."

He smiles at her as though he already knew that and was just teasing. "Of course." He holds out his hand as if to shake. But she doesn't take it. "Come into my office. I'd like to discuss some things with you."

She nods and follows him into a small back office just big enough for one desk and two chairs.

"You must still be very confused about all of this," he says, closing the office door behind them and going to the back of his desk. "I trust your orientation helped you understand some of it?"

"Yeah, I guess." She sits down in the chair opposite him. "So why am I here? Did I do anything wrong?"

He shakes his head. "No, quite the opposite. I'm

hoping that I might be able to convince you into helping us out with something."

"I'm not sure…" she says. "What do you want?"

"It's about Jason Rogers," he says. "He's your boyfriend, correct?"

January nods.

"Did your orientation instructor explain to you how the law works now?"

January shrugs. "Maybe. In all honesty, I wasn't able to follow everything she was talking about. I was still in shock."

Pearson nods and smiles. "Of course. That's completely understandable." He clears his throat. "So incarceration works differently than it did before the time loop. You can't jail anyone if they just disappear from their cells and return to their beds every morning. So it's made the job of a police officer incredibly taxing. We have to re-arrest every criminal and bring them back to jail each and every day. It's not an easy task, I assure you. The trick is to figure out where they sleep, what time they wake up, and capture them while they're still in bed, before they're able to flee."

January nods. It sounds like a ridiculous amount of work, but she can't figure out any other way they could do it.

"But in order to do this, we need people who wake up before the criminals do and live close enough to them to capture them before they get out of bed each morning." Pearson pauses to take a sip of coffee. His face wrinkles up as he drinks, like the coffee was long cold or maybe had some ashes in it. He spits it back in the cup and wipes his mouth. "The problem with your boyfriend is that nobody lives close enough to get to him in time. He's been able to escape us for over a hundred rotations. The last couple of days we've come close, but we need to get him before he wakes up. You live in a decent neighborhood and those who are awake already have good jobs. They don't want to join the police force. I don't blame them. It's a shit job now, even shittier than it was before the loop. But still, we need help. We can't just let a criminal off the hook because he's inconvenient to capture. Our legal system is the only thing that's keeping us from falling into chaos."

"So I hear," January says.

Pearson nods. Then he says, "I know it's a lot to ask, but I'm wondering if you would be interested in restraining your boyfriend each morning during the duration of his sentence. You wouldn't have to officially join the police force, but it would pay fifty dollars a day, deposited directly into your bank account. That doesn't seem like a lot of money, but it adds up. You don't have to pay rent anymore, so that's fifteen hundred dollars a month that you can spend on luxuries. You wouldn't even need to go to your day job anymore if you didn't want to."

"But what am I supposed to do?" January asks. "He's twice my size and I don't own any handcuffs."

He nods. "That's fine. We rarely use handcuffs anymore, anyway. I can teach you how to tie knots using bed sheets or shirts or nylons that will work just as good. You just have to tie him up and wait for my men to arrive. That's all you have to do."

January shakes her head. "I'm sorry, I can't help."

"I know you're loyal to your boyfriend, but trust me—"

She interrupts him, "It's not that. It's just that he wakes up before I do. He'd be long gone before I woke up if he knew I was trying to stop him."

Pearson sighs and nods his head. "Yes, I was worried about that. But it's not impossible. There are methods that you can use to force yourself to wake up sooner. Your dreams are different every night. It's possible to influence your dreams so that they wake you up at an earlier time. For instance, nightmares can cause you to wake up. Some people watch horror movies before bed in order to make this happen. You can also focus on imagining embarrassing situations or thinking about anything that gives you anxiety. If you're willing to at least try, we could really use you."

January looks away, thinking about what he's saying. Then she turns back and says, "But I don't get it. What did Jason do, anyway? He's not a criminal."

The cop sighs and leans back in his chair. "Unfortunately, he's committed one of the most serious crimes in the book."

"What did he do? Kill somebody?"

Pearson shakes his head. "These days, psychological crimes are the worst—the things that don't go away when the day resets. The more psychologically damaging the crime, the harsher the punishment." He pauses to take a deep breath. Then he puts on a serious face. "Your boyfriend is guilty of sexual assault."

January doesn't believe it. "Sexual assault? Do you mean he raped somebody?"

He nods his head. "I'm afraid so. It's a very common crime. There are many men in this society who think they can get away with sexually assaulting women who haven't woken yet. Because, by the next morning, the victim will have forgotten all about it, so they think it's an easy crime to get away with. Some people even feel justified, because they believe there's nothing wrong with committing an act that causes no permanent damage to those they attack."

January just stares at him, not sure what to say. It's got to be a mistake. They have to have the wrong guy. Jason has always had a problem with having sex. He's too shy. He hardly even has sex with her unless he's drunk.

"We get calls every day from not-yet-awake women claiming to have been sexually assaulted. We always have them come in immediately in order to get statements and descriptions of the perpetrators before they go to sleep and forget it all happened, but we very rarely discover the identity of the perpetrator. In this instance, we were lucky, however. The victim was able to ID him."

"So it was somebody he knew? Who was it? Somebody he worked with?"

Pearson shook his head and looked down at his hands.

"I didn't want to have to tell you this, but…" He pauses and takes a deep breath. Then he looks her in the eyes and says, "It was you."

When January hears this, she nearly laughs. She

shakes her head. "That's impossible. I'm his girlfriend. Why would he rape me?"

He shrugs. "I don't know. But you called the police station saying that you were beaten and sexually violated by your boyfriend."

January still doesn't believe it. "But that's not something he'd do. I'm always the one who has to coerce him into having sex. He wouldn't have a reason to rape me."

Pearson shakes his head. "Your boyfriend isn't the same person he was when you knew him. He's been repeating for almost eight years now. Repeating that long will change a man. It can mess with your head, if you're not strong enough. I'm afraid it's turned your boyfriend into a monster."

January doesn't respond. She stares into space. She can't believe Jason would do that to her, no matter the circumstance.

"So will you help us?" Pearson asks.

She takes a moment before responding. When she turns back to him, there's red in her eyes. "I'll help you as long as you look the other way when I beat the fuck out of him."

He smiles. "I'm sorry, but I can't permit that. I understand your desire to get even with him, but please leave that to the authorities. I just want you to try to wake up earlier, restrain him and let us do our job."

She sighs and then nods her head. "Fine."

"But we promise not to go easy on him," he says. "I have a daughter myself. I have no pity for scumbags who prey on women."

That night, January does everything Officer Pearson told her to do. She streams a few horror movies on Netflix with lots of jump scares, all three from a list she'd been given that have been proven to give people nightmares. Most of them are horrible movies and aren't even all that scary. But watching them in the dark, in her bed, with the volume turned all the way up, she can't help but be affected by them. The concepts aren't original and the characters aren't very fleshed out, but there's something about the background score that elevates tension and the jump scares get her every time. She's never liked horror movies that use cheap tactics to scare you, but by the time she goes to sleep she's definitely in a state of high anxiety. She knows her dreams aren't going to be nice ones.

But when January wakes up the next morning, Jason is already awake. He is putting on his pants, trying to move quietly. She knows she won't be able to stop him this time.

"What the fuck, Jason?" she says.

If she's not going to be able to restrain him she's at least going to confront him about what he did.

"Go back to sleep," he says. "I don't want to wrap you up in any of this."

77

She sits up. "They said you raped me, you fucking asshole. What the hell is wrong with you?"

Jason just shakes his head and laughs as he buckles his belt.

"Is *that* what they told you?" he asks.

January gets out of bed.

"Are you going to deny it?" she asks. "What the hell happened to you? They said you've been awake for eight years now. What have you been doing all this time? I don't even know who you are anymore."

Jason sits down and puts on his shoes.

"I didn't do anything to you," he says. "I don't know how to prove it. You just have to believe me."

When he's finished with his shoes, he turns to her.

"Don't believe a single word they say," he tells her. "They don't want me because of that."

"Then why are they after you?"

He shakes his head. "You wouldn't understand."

Before he can leave the room, January gets in his way. "Try me."

He sighs, not wanting to deal with this. But he tells her anyway.

"I've been exploring the neverday," he says. "I think I've found what they're trying to keep hidden. I think I've discovered why all this is happening."

"What the hell are you talking about?" January says.

He shakes his head. "I have to go. If they catch me they're going to kill me."

"So what?" she says. "You can't die anymore."

He pushes her out of the way and explains as she

78

follows him downstairs.

"They kill you in a different way now," he says. "They have ways to torture you to the point of destroying your mind. Psychological torture. Once you go through that, you won't remember anything, not even who you are. *That's* what they're going to do to me if they catch me alive."

"You're full of shit," she says. "You have to be."

"Do you really think they'd send the whole police force after me if I was a common criminal?" he asks. "If they can't catch you right when you wake up they don't bother. But they've been sending everything they've got at me all day, every day, for months now. They don't want me to tell anyone what I know."

Jason runs through her living room and grabs her car keys.

"And what exactly do you know?" she asks, following close behind.

He just shakes his head. "I'm close. Very close."

But he doesn't explain further.

"Don't tell them I told you this or you'll be in danger," he says. "Just play along."

"Are you fucking with me?" she asks.

He shakes his head and says, "Your life depends on it."

Then he rushes out the door and drives off.

Five minutes later, the deputies come asking what happened with Jason. She tells them she didn't wake up early enough to restrain him. They tell her to try harder the next day.

She goes to group therapy, wondering what to believe. On one hand, she knows that Jason is now a completely different person so she doesn't know if she can trust him. But on the other hand, she doesn't think he's capable of doing what they said he did, no matter how long he's been awake. She wonders if there really is some truth to what he told her.

Karl didn't take the bus with her but meets her outside of Room 1803.

"How's it going?" he asks her, hovering around the coffee and doughnut table.

She shakes her head and whispers, "We need to talk."

"About what?" he asks, stuffing a doughnut in his mouth.

"After the session," she says.

He nods and grabs two more doughnuts from the table before going into the room.

As soon as the group starts, Nick narrows in on January.

"Are you willing to start today?" Nick asks her.

She shrugs. "Sure, why not…"

He nods and waits for her to speak, but she doesn't say anything. She's too focused on what her boyfriend had told her that morning. The fact that she's repeating or the fact that she was killed in a car accident—those things seem more trivial than they did the day before. She's more worried about whether or not her boyfriend actually assaulted her or if he's telling the truth about

80

being hunted for what he found in the neverday.

Nick interrupts her thoughts and says, "So the same day you awoke was the day after dying in a car accident. That's got to be a hard way to start your loop. Waking is hard enough, but having to deal with experiencing death is even harder. It's not something that people commonly experience until at least a hundred rotations, if not a few thousand."

January shrugs. "I don't know. I think dying helped a little."

Nick is confused by her statement, but his fake smile doesn't leave his face. "How so?"

"Well, waking up after the accident was kind of a relief," she says. "I thought I was dead. This new world hasn't been an easy thing to wrap my head around, but at least it's given me a second chance at life. So, in a way, I'm kind of thankful for it."

Nick doesn't seem to believe her. He says, "But I've been told that your boyfriend is the one who got you killed. He also sexually abused you during a time before you were awake. Yet you still have to wake up next to him every morning. That's got to be hard."

She nods. "Yeah, I'm trying to wrap my head around that as well. I haven't been able to speak to Jason for more than a few minutes at a time, but he seems to be a completely different person than I remember. They told me yesterday that he assaulted me at some point while he was awake and I wasn't, but of course I don't remember any of that. It doesn't seem possible. He was always such a nice guy."

Nick nods his head. "Yes, it's difficult when you wake at a much later time than your loved ones and discover that they have become different people from who you remember. Many of us have experienced this. It's especially tough if you learn they've become criminals or abusers during this time."

January doesn't know what to say. She's not feeling betrayed or fearful of Jason, just confused about what's really going on. She decides it's best to just play the victim for now, rather than explain how she really feels.

"Luckily, he's gone before I wake up every morning," she says. "Outside of the smell of his cologne he leaves behind, I don't have to deal with him."

Nick nods at her. "This is a good solution for now. Just avoid interacting with him. Eventually, you'll have to confront him for what he did. But there's no rush. You have plenty of time."

January shrugs. She's not actually concerned about her boyfriend. She's more worried about whether or not he's telling the truth.

"So who's next?" Nick asks the group. He looks toward a muscled bald man. "Dwayne, how about you?"

The man shrugs. When January sees him, she thinks it's funny that his name is Dwayne because he kind of looks like a short version of the actor/wrestler Dwayne "The Rock" Johnson.

"Yeah…" he says. "I'm Dwayne and I've been repeating for about seven years now."

Most of the people in the group nod at him, like they know him very well. He must be a regular.

"So, many of you already know that I was in prison when I first woke up. I was only a few months away from being released. But because of the time loop, I had another four years added to my sentence. The warden and many of the guards were awake. They knew what I was going through and knew that I should've been released if time was flowing normally, but they didn't do anything about it. They said their hands were tied. I thought I was doomed to spend all of eternity in prison just because I knocked out a guy who grabbed my girlfriend's ass."

"Good for you," Mitch says. "I would have done the same."

Dwayne just stares down Mitch for saying that. The tattooed kid was only being friendly, but he said the wrong thing. If Dwayne hadn't punched the guy he wouldn't be in the situation he's in now.

"Anyway…" Dwayne continues. "Eventually, they started letting me out. They needed the prison space for day-criminals. So now I'm released every morning, just after breakfast. But it still doesn't feel like I'm free. I still wake up back in my cell every morning. I feel like they don't have to let me out if they don't want to. And if I make one wrong move, piss off the wrong guard, I worry that I'll be stuck in that cell forever." He shrugs. "Basically, freedom doesn't taste so sweet when you know it's temporary. I got a job bagging groceries and work long hours, with no home to go back to at night. It's like I'm just on a work-release program. I'm a prisoner in the morning, a bag boy during the day, and a homeless man at night. Happiness feels like a distant memory."

"But things could be worse," Nick says.

Dwayne shrugs. "Of course it can be worse. But that doesn't help anything. My life still sucks." The man pauses, grinding his teeth. "I've never mentioned this before, but the only thing that helps is when I'm in the neverday."

When he says this, January's eyes light up. She looks up from her lap, paying close attention to him.

"But that's illegal," Nick says.

Dwayne nods. "I know. But when I stay awake long enough to enter the neverday, I don't have to worry about going back to my jail cell. My bank account isn't updated so I can spend as much money as I want. I check into a hotel, eat whatever I want, and live like a king for as long as I can stay awake. One thing people don't tell you is that you get a second wind if you stay awake long enough. You don't feel tired anymore. You might feel weak, but not tired. And uppers help immensely."

Nick shakes his head at Dwayne. "You know I have to report you if you're going into the neverday. It's one of the most serious crimes. You can't do it."

Dwayne shrugs. "Don't worry about it. I don't do it anymore. This was a long time ago. I know it's illegal. I've given it up. But for a while there, I felt like I was actually able to enjoy my life again."

"What changed?" Nick asks. "Why did you stop?"

He says, "Because it lost its appeal. I guess my depression got so bad that nothing was fun anymore. Going into the neverday became too much of a hassle to deal with."

"What was it like?" someone asks.

January looks over to see Lyle, the writer, asking the question. He's just as curious as she is.

"It's exactly how it would be if a tomorrow actually came," Dwayne says. "Everyone who's awake is excited that the time loop has ended. There are parties in the streets. Everyone feels like the nightmare is finally over. It's a good time. You just—"

Nick interrupts him, "We can't talk about this. It's a serious crime." He stares down Dwayne. "Because you're no longer entering the neverday, I won't report this. But you can't tell anyone what it's like. If you say one more word about the neverday I will be forced to tell the authorities. And then you really *will* be forced to spend eternity stuck in your cell."

Dwayne holds up his hands. "Fine. Whatever you say. I'm not recommending anyone go in the neverday, anyway. It's not worth it."

Nick turns away from him, trying to get the conversation away from illegal topics, and says, "Let's give somebody else a turn. Who'd like to go?"

When nobody speaks out, he calls on a middle-aged man with nice clothes and designer shoes.

The new guy is an emergency room doctor who talks about how unfulfilling his job is now that his services are no longer necessary in the new world. He just has to keep people comfortable until the day starts over again. He feels more like a babysitter than a doctor. And anyone in a serious life-threatening condition, he often just lets die because it's easier that way. It's not like they'll die permanently anyway.

But January doesn't care to pay much attention to the doctor. She's more interested in Dwayne and what he had to say about the neverday. She wonders how far into it he's gone. She wonders if he knows as much as her boyfriend knows about it. She wonders if his life is in just as much danger as Jason's.

She hopes that after the meeting that she can talk to Dwayne in private, desperate to know everything he knows about the neverday.

CHAPTER
SIX

Karl spends the whole meeting wondering what January wanted to speak to him about. She seemed pretty upset. But after the meeting is over, she doesn't go to him. Instead, she speaks to the convict, Dwayne, chasing him down the hallway to stop him before he leaves. She seems very adamant about whatever she wants to talk to him about.

At first, Karl feels awkward interrupting their conversation, but he decides to go over to them anyway.

As he approaches, he hears Dwayne saying, "I've got work in an hour. I'm not sure."

"It'll be fine," January says. "It won't take long."

When Karl walks up to them, January turns to him and asks, "Do you want to go out for drinks with us?"

Karl shrugs. "Sure. I don't really have any money, though."

"I'll buy," she says.

After she says this, she attracts the attention of others from the group walking down the hallway toward them.

"Did you say you're going for a drink?" asks Tony, the sweaty bald man who's suffering from a permanent hangover. "Can I go too? I always drink after every meeting anyway."

January shakes her head, but Karl speaks too soon. He says, "Yeah, that would be fun."

And the bald guy nods his head with excitement. The tattooed guy, Mitch, and the writer, Lyle, also seem interested in coming.

"Do you have cash?" Tony asks.

January nods.

"Because if you do I know a place where the bartender hasn't woken up yet," Tony says. "Most bars won't take cash if they suspect you're awake. This place doesn't know any better, so you can use all the cash you want. It's basically like drinking for free."

Karl nods at him. "Sounds good. We should go there."

When they all look at January, she sighs and says, "Fine. I've got two hundred dollars in cash. I'll buy."

Mitch and Lyle cheer with excitement and pat the woman on the back. Then the six of them follow Tony outside, heading several blocks down the road to the only bar in town with free beer.

When they get there, the place is packed. It appears that a lot of people know about the bar that still accepts cash. And a lot of people are really interested in the idea of beer they can buy with their ever-recycling amount of pocket cash.

They take the only table available, but it doesn't look like they're going to be served any time soon. The bartender is in a panic, not knowing what to do with so many customers. He's obviously not used to having this many people in his bar at once and wasn't expecting such a rush. Since he's not awake yet, he has no idea that it's probably like this each and every rotation.

"So what do you want to talk about?" Karl asks January, after they sit down at the table.

A look of concern spreads across her face. She wasn't expecting so many people to be a part of the discussion.

"Can I trust all of you?" January asks.

Lyle, Tony, and Mitch look at each other, not sure what she's talking about.

"I wanted to talk to you about the neverday," she says.

When she says this, Dwayne moans and gets up to leave.

"Wait…" she says, pulling him back down. "I need to talk about this."

Dwayne sits back down, but looks annoyed. He doesn't want to have to deal with this. He just wants to go back to work.

"So I don't really know any of you very well," January says. "So what I have to say doesn't leave this table."

Karl nods, but the others seem confused.

"So we're not just here to get drunk?" Tony asks. "Because that's all I'm here for."

January shakes her head. She pulls her wallet out of

her purse and hands it to Tony. "Just order us a round."

Tony doesn't argue. He grabs two hundred bucks out of her wallet and goes to the bar.

The others are all interested. Mitch and Lyle are also newcomers, so they are craving new information about their new world just as much as Karl is.

"So, my boyfriend is on the run," January tells them. "They say that he's a rapist and needs to be brought to justice, but I don't think that's true. He told me that it's because he's been exploring the neverday."

Dwayne nods his head. "That's probably true. As you saw in group today, none of the old ones want you talking about the neverday."

"Old ones?" Mitch asks.

"That's what we call people who have been repeating for a really long time. Some of them are hundreds of years old now."

Karl laughs and shakes his head at the thought. He's been repeating for thousands of years. These *old ones* are mere children as far as he's concerned.

Dwayne continues, "They don't like anyone exploring the neverday. And I'm inclined to agree. It's better to forget it even exists."

January nods at him, but appears slightly disappointed in his words. It's like she hoped he'd have more answers for her than that.

"I think there's something to it," January says.

"Like what?" Lyle asks.

"I don't know," she says. "He told me that he found something there. He believes that there's an answer to why we're repeating. Something that explains why all of this is happening."

Dwayne shakes his head. "I've stayed awake for five days straight and there's nothing there that you want to see. It's just a bunch of days that disappear after you go to sleep."

January shrugs. "I don't know. He sounded serious about it. What if he really found something?"

"Like what?" Karl asks.

"I don't know…" January says. "But I can't stop thinking about it."

Tony returns with a tray containing six shots of whiskey and six pints of beer. His breath already smells like whiskey, like he already took a couple shots while he was at the bar.

"What is this?" Lyle asks, frowning after he takes a sip of the beer.

"Hamm's," Tony says.

"Hamm's?" Lyle says in an angry tone. "Are you kidding me?"

"It's on sale for three fifty," Tony says.

"Didn't they have an IPA?"

"Yeah, for like six bucks or more," Tony says.

"But it's three times the alcohol and actually tastes good," Lyle says. "Hamm's is just piss water."

Tony shrugs and chugs his beer. "It's free beer. Just drink it."

Nobody else seems to care. They take their drinks

and sip them casually. When Karl drinks his, memories flow back into his head. He doesn't remember what beer tasted like. The Hamm's isn't exactly delicious, but the carbonation and alcohol hits his palette pleasantly. He's happy to have it. It's like a new experience, like he's having his first beer all over again.

"Why don't we go there and see for ourselves?" Mitch asks.

Tony doesn't know what he's talking about, but some of the others get nervous by his words.

"Where?" Tony asks.

"To the neverday?" Lyle asks.

"Yeah, why not?" Mitch asks. "I've got a shitload of cocaine. Enough for my whole band for a whole tour. We could stay awake for days with it."

Dwayne shakes his head, "You don't want to go there. It's not worth it."

"But why not try?" Mitch asks. "It could be fun."

Dwayne isn't interested. He takes a shot of whiskey and says, "I just admitted that I've been in the neverday. They're going to be watching me. I shouldn't even be in this conversation right now."

Unlike Dwayne, Karl seems very interested in this idea.

"What would we even be looking for?" he asks.

"I don't know yet," January says. "In the morning, I'll talk to my boyfriend and try to get more information out of him. It could be as simple as a news story on television that explains why there was a time loop in the first place."

"Let's do it," Mitch says. "What's the worst that can happen?"

"You can be locked up for eternity," Dwayne says.

Mitch shrugs. "I wake up on a tour bus driving through town each morning. They'll never catch me. I don't even have a home address anymore."

Dwayne shakes his head. "Whatever you want to do is fine by me. Just leave me out of it."

He takes a long chug of his beer, then stands up. "I've got to go to work."

"Are you sure?" January asks him. "We could use your help."

Dwayne shakes his head. "I don't want any part of this. I just want to keep my head down and stay out of trouble. Maybe you all have a chance to escape the law, but I already wake up in a cell. If I break the laws, I'm fucked."

He stands up and says, "Good luck to you all. Don't talk to me again."

And leaves the bar.

Everyone else seems interested in the idea of exploring the neverday. Mitch, Lyle, and January are all new to repeating, so they have a good reason for being curious. Karl is interested just because anything new is exciting to him. He doesn't care about breaking any laws. There's nothing that they can do that will be any worse than what he's been doing to himself for thousands of years. He could always go back to killing himself every morning to avoid being arrested if he has to.

Tony is the only person with any reservations besides Dwayne, but even he's a little turned on by the idea.

"If I stayed awake long enough, the hangover would probably wear off," Tony says.

"Especially if you were doing coke," Mitch says.

He nods. "I'll try it, I guess. If I can feel what it's like to be sober for even a moment, it would all be worth it."

"When should we start?" Lyle asks.

"Not tonight," Mitch says. "My band already left town without me and they've got the coke. How about tomorrow?"

They all nod in agreement.

"I'll talk to my boyfriend in the morning," January says. "We meet up after the meeting and then try to stay awake and see what we can find out."

"It'll probably take many tries before we learn anything," Karl says.

January nods. "Then we keep trying. I don't know about you, but I want to know why this is happening to us. I don't care about the consequences, especially if there's a way to stop it."

"Do you really think there's a way to stop it?" Lyle asks.

January shrugs. "I don't know, but figuring out why it's happening is the first step to figuring out how to end it."

They all nod and drink their beers. Karl smiles at the group of people at the table. It's been so long since he's been a part of a group of people with goals and aspirations that he can't help but get excited about their future.

"Mind if we keep drinking until our cash runs out?" Tony asks January.

She nods her head. "Sure. We've got nothing else to do before tomorrow, anyway." Then she turns to Mitch. "Are you sure you can get the cocaine?"

Mitch nods. "I just need to grab the bag and hop out at a stoplight. My bandmates will freak out but they won't chase after me. Since they aren't awake, they won't know what the hell is happening."

"Don't fuck up," January says.

Mitch just smiles, completely confident that he'll pull through for them.

CHAPTER
SEVEN

January spends the whole night watching horror movies and trying to put herself into a heightened state of anxiety so that she can wake up before her boyfriend. But she doesn't do it in order to get Jason arrested. She just wants to make sure she can wake up with plenty of time to pick his brain about everything he knows about the neverday.

When she wakes up the next morning, a smile stretches across her face as she feels him lying in bed next to her. She finally woke up before he did. But she's not sure why. She didn't have any nightmares that pulled her out of sleep. When she looks at her clock, she notices that there's five minutes until her alarm normally goes off, which is ten minutes later than she woke up the day before. She wonders why Jason isn't awake yet. He is usually up by now.

January turns to him and says, "Jason? Are you awake?"

There's no response. She shakes him, but he doesn't wake. When she pulls the cover off of him, she recoils in shock. His body is covered in blue welts. A look of terror distorts his face. Jason is dead.

January jumps out of bed and steps away from him. She has no idea what could have happened. She remembers the last thing he told her about how the authorities have a way to kill people permanently. She wonders if that's what happened to him. But then she remembers that he said the way they kill people is by destroying their brain through psychological torture. If that's what happened, then he would still be alive. He would just be a rambling idiot or a comatose vegetable. He wouldn't actually be dead.

January leaves the room and waits for the authorities to arrive.

The guy with the beard and his older partner show up first. She tells them he's upstairs. But when they go up there and see his dead body, they're just as freaked out by it as she is.

"What the heck happened to him?" asks the bearded man, still pointing his shotgun at the body even though there's no reason for it.

"I don't know," January says, her back turned so that she doesn't have to see it.

"Did you do this?" the older man asks.

January shakes her head. "He was like that when I woke up."

"But what's with the blue stuff?" asks the bearded man.

January looks and sees that the blue welts are leaking a strange glowing fluid.

She shrugs at him. "How the hell should I know?"

"We need to call this in," says the older man.

"I didn't do it," January says.

"I didn't say you did," he replies.

"How did it happen?" January asks.

The man shrugs. "We'll wait until Paul arrives. Maybe he'll know."

When Paul Pearson arrives at the house, they take him upstairs to look at Jason's body. He only examines it for a few seconds before he nods his head and covers the body with a bed sheet.

"He's gone," Pearson says. "There's nothing we can do."

But January isn't satisfied by his words.

"What do you mean?" she asks.

Pearson tells her, "It's an unusual occurrence but it happens from time to time. Some people just wake up dead."

"But he didn't just wake up dead," January says. "Look at him. Something happened. It's like somebody murdered him." She points at his covered body. "And what were those blue welts? What caused that?"

Pearson looks her in the eyes. In a serious tone, he says, "We don't know. But I've seen this a few times before.

Some people just die like this and never come back."

"What do you mean they never come back?" January asks.

But Pearson doesn't respond. He turns to his men and says, "Let's go. There's nothing we can do here."

The bearded man and the older guy nod and leave the room.

"Where are you going?" January asks. "You're just going to leave his body here?"

Pearson nods at her. "I'm sorry, but we've got more pressing matters. There's nothing more to do here."

"But—" January begins.

"You don't have to worry about him anymore," Pearson says, not interested in anything else she has to say. "He'll never hurt you again."

Before he explains anything else to her, he goes downstairs and leaves the house, abandoning her with her boyfriend's horrific corpse lying in her bed.

After the therapy session, January meets the four men she planned to enter the neverday with and tells them, "Let's wait another day."

"But why?" Mitch asks. "I got the coke and everything."

"My boyfriend was dead when I woke up this morning," she says. "I didn't get any information out of him."

Karl is the only one who is understanding. "We don't have to stay awake if you're not ready."

"Fuck that," Mitch says. "I want to see what happens."

"Yeah," Lyle says. "We should at least try it out. We already know that it will take multiple attempts before we learn anything."

Tony says, "I don't even care about learning why we're repeating. I just want to see what it feels like to get over my hangover. Let's do it."

January lets out a long sigh and says, "Fine. Whatever."

"You can always ask your boyfriend about it later," Karl says. "You know, once the day starts over again."

January agrees, but she's still concerned over why he died in the first place. She wishes she would have gotten more information out of him when she had the chance.

The five of them hang out downtown all day. They focus on doing physical activities to keep themselves awake, walking through the streets and eating snacks whenever they find a street vendor willing to take cash. They don't break into the coke until late at night, once they're too tired to keep going.

Sitting in a cheap hotel room, chopping lines of coke—the bed filled with fleas, the bathtub stained brown for some reason, the sink covered in long human hair like some woman just shaved her head and left it there.

"Why'd we get such a shithole of a room?" Lyle asks. "It's late enough at night that our bank accounts won't be charged. We could have gotten a nicer place."

January shakes her head and snorts a line. She hasn't put anything up her nose since high school and the act is bringing back horrible memories of late night meth-fueled philosophical debates and making out with skeazy guys.

"We don't want a room we'd feel comfortable in," she says. "There's no chance we'll fall asleep in a shithole like this."

Tony chuckles and takes the rolled twenty dollar bill from January. "I don't know. I can sleep anywhere."

"Yeah, I've slept in worse," Mitch says, speaking lightning-fast and grinding his teeth between pauses. "But I'm good at staying awake. When I was a kid, I used to play a game with my brothers to see who could stay awake the longest. It was in the summer when we didn't have to go to school. We'd stay up for days at a time and I'd always last the longest. I think five days is my record."

"We might have to stay awake for longer than five days," January says.

"Do we have enough coke for that?" Tony asks.

Mitch nods. "We have enough for at least a week."

"We'll probably need enough for two weeks," January says.

"Two weeks?" Tony asks. "How the hell can you possibly go without sleep for two weeks?"

"It's possible," Lyle says. "I've read articles online about people who swear they haven't slept for several years."

Tony shakes his head. "That's impossible. You'd die."

Lyle shrugs. "I don't know. If we could learn to live without sleep we wouldn't have to deal with repeating every day."

"But how shitty of a life would that be?" Tony says.

"It can't be any worse than being as hungover as you are every day," Lyle says.

Tony shrugs and does another line, out of turn.

The only one who isn't completely wired is Karl, who hasn't taken a line yet. His eyes are rolling back, his consciousness beginning to fade.

"You need some of this," Mitch tells him.

Karl sits up, slaps himself awake. "No, I'm good."

"You're going to fall asleep."

Karl shakes his head, nearly passing out in the process.

"Come on, man," Mitch says. "Our job is to keep each other awake. We're not letting you pass out on us."

Mitch puts the rolled twenty in his face and shoves it into his nose.

Karl just flicks it out.

"Have you never done this before?" January asks him.

Karl shrugs. "Maybe. I don't remember."

"It's no big deal," she says. "It's not like it'll kill you."

Karl says, "Yeah, but will it really keep you awake for so long? I know that caffeine makes you crash harder once it wears off. This stuff has to be even worse."

Mitch shakes his head. "As long as you keep doing it, you'll be fine. Trust me."

Karl takes the money straw and looks down at the line of powder.

"Can't I just put it in a soda and drink it?" he asks.

Mitch shakes his head. "It wouldn't be as effective. Just snort it."

When he attempts to snort the line, Karl somehow misses. He just scoops the coke into the straw, only getting a few granules up his nose. When he pulls back, his nostrils wiggle like something up there is tickling his nose hairs.

Just before Karl sneezes, Mitch leaps over the table, using his leather jacket as a shield. Karl blows snot all over his back, but the cocaine is safe.

They all laugh.

"That would have been a disaster," January says.

Karl wipes his nose. His face turns red.

"Sorry," Karl says. "I have bad allergies. I can't really breathe through my nose."

Mitch takes off his jacket and rubs the slime on the carpet.

"Okay, you don't have to snort it," Mitch says in an annoyed tone.

Karl inches back, completely embarrassed by making a spectacle of himself.

"Just rub it on your gums," January says.

"Why do people rub coke on their gums, anyway?" Lyle asks. "I've never understood that. Why not just eat it?"

January shrugs. "It hits the bloodstream faster, I think."

Karl licks his finger and presses it against his line. Then he puts it in his mouth and rubs his gums. Most of it falls between his teeth and under his tongue, but he does what he can. Even though he's supposed to be thousands of years old, he looks like a kid as he does it.

Everyone laughs at his awkwardness, but he goes through with it anyway. It takes him twice as long to get through his line. When it's over, he spends the next hour licking the roof of his mouth and rubbing his gums.

January can't help but think of him as an innocent little kid just trying drugs for the first time. It's kind of adorable.

For days, they stay awake, living out of that hotel room. They take a line every three hours and go for as many walks as possible per day, to keep their blood pumping. Most of them are getting cranky and delirious and high-strung, but they keep on going.

There doesn't seem to be any answers, though. They watch the news every chance they get, but it's mostly just normal stories about police shootings and the latest presidential embarrassment, as though the time loop never happened.

"This isn't getting us anywhere," Lyle says after they turn off the television in their grungy hotel room. "Maybe we should give up."

January shakes her head. "I'm not giving up. My boyfriend seemed sure of it."

"He could have gone crazy," Tony says. "That happens a lot to people now. The asylums are packed full of day-lunatics."

"Maybe…" January says. "But I don't think so. I'm sure there's something we're not seeing."

They do more lines of coke and watch more television.

"Maybe we should go to the university," Karl says.

They all look at him.

"Why the university?" January asks.

Karl shrugs. "The people in the neverday believe the time loop has ended, even though it's a false reality. There's got to be people who are trying to figure out why it all happened. The university might be a good place to start."

"But why the university?" Lyle asks. "College professors don't know shit. It's not like they actually do anything but fuck their students."

Karl dismisses the writer's comment. He rubs coke into his gums and then looks up. "If they're not researching the phenomenon themselves, they might know who is. It's worth checking out."

The others look at each other and shrug.

"We got nothing better to do," Mitch says.

"We'll go in the morning," January says.

They spend the rest of the night researching the layout of the university online, looking for the right department. None of them believe this will result in anything, but it will likely keep them awake. They don't know what they're looking for, but they know staying awake is the most important thing they can do.

CHAPTER
EIGHT

Karl Lybeck has to pry the other people off the hotel room floor in order to get them to go to the university. They have been up for six days straight, running exclusively on cocaine, and are now finding it difficult to move.

"We need another line before we go," Mitch says.

When he pulls out his baggy, he realizes he's almost out.

"Fuck…" he says. "We're going to need more. There's only enough for half a line each."

"I thought you said we had enough for at least a week," January says. "It hasn't even been one week yet."

Mitch shrugs. "We must have hit it too hard. This much would've lasted my band all month."

"Can we get more?" January asks.

Mitch shakes his head. "I'm not from around here. I don't know any dealers."

"Then what are we going to do?" Tony asks. "I'm loving this shit. I haven't felt this good in a long ass time."

"We should go to the black side of town," Mitch says.

"We'll surely be able to score some coke there."

Lyle's eyebrows curl in disgust. "That's racist as fuck, man."

Mitch shrugs. "Yeah, but it works. My band does that all the time when we're on tour. It's the best way to get drugs when you don't know anyone in town."

Lyle just shakes his head. "You're such an asshole…"

"Fine," Mitch says. "Where's the white trash side of town? We'll be able to get meth there. It's cheaper and stronger anyway. Would that make you feel less racist?"

Lyle just rolls his eyes.

"We should just ask Dwayne," January says. "He said he knew how to get stuff on the street. We'll just have to track him down."

"I wish he would have stayed up with us," Tony says. "I don't know how the heck we'll find the guy."

"He works at a grocery store somewhere around here," January says. "We'll find him."

Karl shakes his head at the others. "Let's just go to the university. We'll figure out how to stay awake later."

"We could just drink a shitload of coffee," Lyle says. "Or energy drinks. Cocaine isn't much different than drinking a shitload of caffeine."

"Let's just go," Karl says. "We'll worry about it later."

The others agree. They finish off the last of the coke and put their shoes on, then head out of the cheap motel.

They wait at the bus stop for over an hour, but the bus never comes.

"It's not far," Lyle says. "We should just walk."

"I'm beat, man," Tony argues. "My bones feel like they're falling apart. I don't think I'll make it on foot."

"The walk will be good for you. Let's go." Then Lyle heads off down the road, leaving the others at the bus stop.

"The bus will come eventually," Tony says.

But nobody listens to him. They follow after Lyle.

The streets are dead. No cars are driving on the road. No people are walking on the sidewalks.

"What time is it?" January asks. "The place is quiet."

"I haven't seen a single person yet," Lyle says.

Karl looks at his watch. "It's nine-thirty."

"What day is it?" Lyle asks. "Is it Sunday? Downtown would only be this dead on a Sunday."

Karl shakes his head. "It's Tuesday."

Lyle looks around, unable to believe what he's seeing. "Tuesday? The streets should be crowded on a Tuesday."

"It's the neverday," January says. "Who knows what people are doing now? For all we know, they declared a week-long holiday to celebrate being free of the time loop."

Lyle shakes his head. "It's still weird. There's not even any homeless people."

But just as he says this, they pass an alley and see a homeless man in a sleeping bag, passed out next to a dumpster.

"There's a homeless guy," January says, pointing into the alley. "People are just sleeping in."

Lyle nods and keeps walking.

"It's kind of nice being the only people on the road," Mitch says. "I hate being around people when I've been on a coke binge this long, anyway."

"You're still around us," Tony says.

Mitch shrugs. "It's fine if I'm around other people who have been doing it with me." He spits onto the sidewalk. "Actually, it's far better than doing it alone."

The others nod and keep walking. They don't bother waiting for the *walk* sign whenever they come to an intersection. There's no one driving who could possibly hit them. Besides the one sleeping homeless man, they don't come across another living soul.

When they get to the university, there's no difference. Nobody is out and about. It's now after ten in the morning and there's not a single student walking around campus.

"Are all the classes in session or something?" Lyle asks.

January shakes her head. "Even if they were, there'd still be kids all over the place. This place is deader than it is during winter break."

They go from building to building, but there's no one to be found. The classrooms are all empty. The administration building is locked. The science labs are covered in dust.

"What the hell's going on?" Mitch asks. "This place is a graveyard."

"Let's try the dorms," January says.

They all agree and go for the tallest co-ed dorm on campus.

The lobby door is unlocked, but the interior is as dead as anywhere else on campus. They go up a floor and try the rooms. Most of the doors are locked, but they find one that's open near the end of the hallway.

January knocks before entering.

"Hello?" she asks.

No answer.

They step inside. There are two beds in the room, both occupied by sleeping students.

"Hello?" January says again. "Are you asleep?"

But it's obvious they're both asleep.

The others wait in the doorway as Karl and January approach the two sleeping students.

January touches the one on the far side of the room.

"Are you okay?" she asks, pushing on the person on the bed. "Wake up."

But the student doesn't wake.

"Are they dead?" Lyle asks.

January shrugs.

When Karl goes to the other one, he feels the student's neck.

"The pulse is weird," he says. "It's really fast." He steps back. "And his skin is ice cold."

January touches the student near her and nods her head. "Same here."

"What the fuck?" Mitch says. He steps into the room and examines the two students.

"Their skin is wet," Karl says. "But it's not sweat. It's more like..." He touches the student again. "It's like slime."

"We should go," Lyle says.

Mitch touches one of them to see what Karl is talking about. The second he feels the flesh, he pulls away and wipes the slime on his pants.

"This is fucked up," Mitch says. "Let's get out of here." The others agree.

They go to other rooms in the dormitory with unlocked doors and find the same thing. More students covered in slimy sweat with rapid pulses and freezing cold skin.

"Why is this happening?" Mitch asks.

"It has something to do with the neverday," January says. "It has to."

"Maybe we should just go to sleep and forget this ever happened," Lyle says.

But Karl shakes his head. He's as excited as he's been in as long as he can remember.

"No," he says. "This is just starting to get interesting."

The others look at him.

Karl says, "We've got to stay awake and see why this is happening."

Lyle and Tony don't seem to agree. They shake their

heads, terrified of what's going on. But January and Mitch share his enthusiasm.

"I think we're getting close to the answer," January says.

Mitch goes to the dorm room medicine cabinet, searching through the contents.

"Here we go," he says, holding up a bottle of prescription medication. "Ritalin. This will keep us awake."

"I thought Ritalin slows you down," January says.

Mitch shakes his head. "No, it's basically speed. If you have ADD it will regulate you if you take it for a while, but for everyone else it's almost as good as doing coke. We can stay awake for days on this stuff."

Karl and January nod at him.

"But do we really want to stay awake?" Lyle asks. "This is getting too fucked up."

Tony nods in agreement. "Yeah, I think I've had enough fun. I'd rather just go back to repeating."

Mitch shakes his head at them.

"We're only just getting started," he says, twisting the lid off of the bottle and popping three tiny pills in his mouth.

The others look at him as he pours half a dozen pills into his palm and holds them out for them.

January nods. "Let's do it."

She grabs a pill and pops it into her mouth. Karl follows her lead. But Lyle and Tony hesitate. They shake their heads. This whole ordeal isn't fun for them anymore.

They spend the entire day trying to find somebody else who's awake, but every single person is the same as the students they found in the dorm. The homeless people sleeping on the sidewalks have the same cold slimy skin and rapid pulse.

"It's everyone," January says, standing over a homeless man. "What the hell is wrong with them?"

Karl says, "They're not dead. They're sick or something."

Tony notices a stray cat sleeping behind a dumpster with the same symptoms.

"It's the animals, too," he says.

January looks around. "Yeah, I haven't seen even birds in the sky. Every living creature seems to be affected."

"But what does this have to do with the time loop?" Tony asks. "It doesn't make sense."

They stand in place, thinking about it, rubbing their sweaty foreheads.

"Maybe it's a disease that wipes out all life on earth," Lyle says.

They all look at him.

"One of the most popular theories is that we're repeating because the world is about to end." He points at the sleeping homeless man. "Maybe it's because of a disease."

"Seriously?" January asks, a smirk crawling up her face. "You actually believe there's some kind of higher alien intelligence that put the time loop in place to save us from extinction?"

Lyle shrugs. "Aliens, God, secret government scientists... I don't know..."

"But if it's a disease it wouldn't affect everyone at once like this," Karl says. "Everyone was fine last night. If a plague swept through, we would have gotten it, too. But outside of being tired and medicated, I feel just fine."

"So do I," January says.

"Then what is happening?" Lyle asks.

But they just look at each other. Nobody has any idea.

"So should we just go back to the hotel and go to sleep?" Tony asks.

The others shrug.

"I don't know what else to do," Lyle says.

But before they're able to make up their minds, they hear a car engine roaring down the road.

"What the hell is that?" Mitch asks, listening carefully.

"It's a car..." January says. A smile stretches across her face. "Somebody else is still awake."

They leave the alleyway and rush toward the sound of the vehicle. When they see it, they can't believe their eyes. It's a police vehicle moving slowly through the streets like it's on patrol.

Lyle and Tony rush toward it, waving their arms to get its attention. But the others stay back. The windows are tinted. There's something odd about the way it moves.

The car stops when it sees the two men rush in

front of it.

"You're not sick like the others," Tony yells at the car.

"What the hell is going on?" Lyle asks.

The car just stays in place, revving its engine like it's considering whether or not it should run them over.

Karl can tell there's something not quite right about the cop car. It's like it doesn't belong there. When he looks at the worried expression on January's face, he can tell she's thinking the same thing.

"Get away from it," January yells.

Tony and Lyle look back at her. The person in the cop car doesn't say anything. He just keeps revving his engine.

"We should just bail," Mitch says to Karl.

Karl looks at the tattooed kid. He's inching deeper into the alleyway, ready to take off with or without the others. Karl wonders if the kid has the same eerie feeling about the cop car as he does or if this is just how he always acts around the police.

"But maybe he knows why everyone is asleep…" Lyle calls back to January.

A wave of distortion rings in their ears as the police officer turns on a megaphone.

"The neverday is strictly prohibited to civilians," the officer's voice echoes through the megaphone. "You are ordered to go to sleep immediately and turn yourself in to the authorities on the next rotation. Failure to comply will result in severe disciplinary action."

Lyle and Tony hesitate. They look back at January and then at the cop car, not sure what to do.

"Run for it!" Mitch cries, then turns and runs down the alley.

Only Lyle listens to him. He takes off running toward the alley, passing Karl and January, leaving the fat, middle-aged man in his dust.

Tony doesn't know how to react. He just stands there, looking back at the others. Not sure what to do. He's so out of shape that he probably wouldn't be able to catch up if he ran.

Before he takes a step, the cop leaps out of his cruiser and shoots Tony in the neck.

January screams when she sees him fall. But he wasn't hit with a bullet. The cop's weapon was silent. He fired a tranquilizer dart. He's not trying to kill anyone, he just wants to put them to sleep in order to take them out of the neverday.

When the cop turns to January and Karl, they both recognize him. It's Paul Pearson. The officer they both met in Karl's backyard after January's boyfriend was murdered.

"Let's go!" January cries, covering her face as she turns to run. "Don't let him see you. If he recognizes us, we're fucked."

The cop car speeds down the alley after them, running over trash cans and nearly crushing the comatose homeless man lying in his sleeping bag near the dumpster. Karl and January follow Lyle and Mitch as they exit the alleyway and turn onto the street.

"Do you think there's more of them out there?" Karl asks January as they run, worried that they'll soon be surrounded by an army of neverday cops.

January doesn't respond. She looks behind her as they race down the street, but there aren't any other cop cars. As far as they know, Pearson is the only person out there with them.

Mitch and Lyle get off the street and turn down another alleyway on the opposite side of the street.

"What the fuck are you guys doing?" January yells up to them, but the two men are too far away to hear.

She looks at Karl and says, "That's a dead end. We can't go that way."

Karl nods. "Let's keep going and lead the cop away from them."

She agrees.

But the cop doesn't follow January and Karl as they run in a different direction. He goes after Mitch and Lyle. He parks his cruiser in front of the alley, blocking their only exit.

Karl and January duck into a convenience store and hide.

"We should go back and help them," January says.

Karl shrugs at her as he tries to catch his breath.

"But how?" he asks.

"We rush him," January says. "His tranquilizer gun won't be fast enough to get all of us. Our only chance is to take him down as a group or he'll pick us off one by one."

"But won't he recognize us if we get too close?" Karl asks. "He doesn't know Mitch and Lyle, but he'll be able to identify us if he sees our faces. We won't be safe next time we wake up."

January shrugs. "We'll get him from behind, then. It doesn't matter. He probably already saw our faces anyway."

Karl thinks about it for a second and then nods and smiles.

"Yeah, it'll be fun," he says, realizing that this might just be the most exciting thing that's happened to him in thousands of years. "Let's do it."

Karl and January grab two 22 ounce beer bottles from the refrigerated section of the convenience store and rush toward the alley where Officer Pearson has Lyle and Mitch pinned down.

"There's nowhere else to go," Pearson says through the megaphone. "Come out peacefully with your hands up."

Karl sneaks up behind the cop car and peeks into the alleyway. Lyle and Mitch are hiding behind a dumpster, not able to run any farther. He looks back at January hiding behind the building and nods at her. She keeps her head down as she creeps up next to him behind the cop car.

"This is your last chance," Pearson says.

But the two hiding men don't give themselves up.

The cop gets out of his car and walks down the

alleyway toward them. He aims his tranquilizer pistol, waiting for them to show themselves.

"Don't shoot," Lyle says from behind the dumpster. "We just want to know what the fuck is going on."

But the cop doesn't listen to him.

He says, "Come out slowly. Show yourself."

January and Karl step out from behind the police car and sneak up behind Pearson, wielding their beer bottles like hammers. The glass is freezing against Karl's skin.

"It's over," Pearson says. "Just give up."

As he says this, Lyle and Mitch step out from behind the dumpster with their hands raised. But Mitch has no intention of giving up. He sees January and Karl sneaking up behind the cop and nods at them, then acts as a diversion. He lowers his hands and takes off running toward the back of the alley even though it ends in a brick wall.

Pearson fires a dart at Mitch as the punk runs. It hits him in the leather jacket and he stumbles to the ground.

Before Pearson is able to reload, January lunges at him. She hits him in the back of the head with her beer bottle, foamy brown liquid and shards of glass spray across the cop's shoulders as he falls to the ground. Karl rushes at the cop and kicks away the tranquilizer gun. Then the two of them jump on top of Pearson and pin him to the ground.

Lyle stays in place, keeping his hands in the air.

"Get some handcuffs," January tells him.

"What?" Lyle asks, confused by the whole situation. "Where?"

119

"The car," she tells him. "He'll have handcuffs in the car."

Lyle nods and runs for the cop car.

Pearson struggles beneath them. He's weakened by the blow but still conscious. Blood leaks down his neck.

"You don't know what you're doing," Pearson says. "You've got it all wrong."

"How do we have it wrong?" she asks. "What's going on here?"

"The neverday isn't what you think," he says.

When Lyle returns with the handcuffs, they slap them on his wrists and get him to his feet.

"How's Mitch?" January asks.

They look back at the punk kid who's stepping toward them. He points at the dart in his coat. The needle pierced the flap of his jacket but missed his flesh.

"I'm fine," Mitch says. "It didn't even graze me."

Karl holds Pearson by his elbow and looks at January.

"What now?" he asks her.

She nods back at him. "Let's find a room somewhere. I've got a lot of questions for this guy."

Lyle and Mitch take the cop car to retrieve Tony's body, as Karl and January break into a nearby apartment above the convenience store. They drag Pearson into the apartment and set him down in a chair. January uses the knotting techniques the cop taught her to tie him down, fastening his arms and legs to the chair.

There are two comatose women lying in the king size bed in the center of the studio apartment. When the cop sees them, a look of terror crosses his face.

"We can't stay here," he says. "We have to go to sleep. It's not safe."

When Lyle and Mitch return with Tony's body, they lay him down in the bed next to the two women.

"He's dead asleep," Lyle says about Tony. "We couldn't wake him up. He's gone."

January nods. "Well, at least we didn't leave him in the road."

"And look what I found," Mitch says with excitement on his face, holding out a handful of syringes he got from the cop car.

"What are those?" January asks.

"Adrenalin shots," he says. "It's far more effective than cocaine. We can stay up for days with this."

Officer Pearson shakes his head. His mind is foggy as he speaks, as though he's on the verge of passing out. Karl wonders if January gave him a concussion when she hit him with the beer bottle.

"You don't want to stay awake any longer," Pearson says. "The neverday isn't safe."

When Mitch hears him say this, he looks at January and Karl with a confused face. "What the hell is he talking about?"

January shrugs. "He keeps saying that, but he won't explain why."

"Just trust me," Pearson says, his head rolling from shoulder to shoulder. "You need to go to sleep."

Mitch holds up the cop's tranquilizer gun. "Should I knock him out?"

January shakes her head. "No, I want him awake. We still have a lot to learn."

Karl goes to the three sleeping people on the bed. He examines Tony. His body is sweating profusely. He touches the man's neck and then jumps away from him.

"What's wrong?" January asks.

"He's the same as the others now," Karl says. "He has the same rapid pulse."

"It happens when we sleep," Pearson says. "It happens to all of us."

"What's causing it?" January asks.

Pearson shrugs. "Fuck if I know. It only happens during the neverday."

"Is it some kind of disease?" Lyle asks him. "It looks like a disease."

"I think so…" Pearson says, having trouble holding his head upright. "Once we go to sleep we never wake up again. We just incubate…"

"You don't really know anything, do you?" January asks. "Have you ever stayed awake longer than this? What else happens in the neverday?"

He shakes his head, his eyes rolling in the sockets. "Just shoot me. Kill me. Knock me out. I don't want to be here anymore. I just want to wake up back in my bed with my wife…"

"My boyfriend said that the answer to all of this is in the neverday," January says. "I think I'm beginning to believe him. There's something here that you're not telling us."

The cop squints his eyes as blood leaks down his forehead. "Jan Brady?" He says this as though he only just now recognizes her. "You've got to stop this… You're going to be in so much trouble… You don't understand…"

"Then help me understand," January says.

Before he speaks again, the three bodies on the bed begin to quiver. At first, they begin to mildly shake, but then the bodies thrash about like they are in serious pain.

"What's happening?" Lyle asks.

The four of them step away from the bed as the bodies go into seizure.

"Kill me!" the cop cries, fighting against his bonds. "Quickly!"

They look at the cop as panic explodes from his face.

"This is fucked…" Mitch says, keeping his eyes on the bodies.

"We need to die or go to sleep," the cop says. "It's the only way to escape."

"What's wrong with them?" Lyle asks.

"It's not them," the cop says. "It's what's *inside* of them."

As Pearson says this, the bodies stop moving. They go limp. Then their abdomens split open and black tentacles curl out of their flesh.

"What the fuck is that!" Mitch cries.

The creatures pull themselves out of the three corpses on the bed. Tony's body is torn apart and discarded like loose clothing as the tentacled beast crawls out of him, staring at the people in the room with glowing blue eyes. It's a small alien creature with razor-sharp fangs that hisses and growls at them.

"Kill me, now!" Pearson shrieks. "Don't let them get me!"

The creature emerging from Tony's corpse leaps into the air at Lyle. It wraps its tentacles around him, choking him, and bites into his neck. Lyle screams and pushes against the creature, but it doesn't let him go. It seems to suck the life out of him, draining blood and energy from his flesh.

Mitch shoots a dart from the cop's tranquilizer gun, but it seems to have no effect on the creature. It just bounces off the thing's oily black flesh.

"Untie me!" Pearson yells. "Kill me!"

The other creatures seem to be attracted to the cop's screams. They jump from the bed toward him, wrapping around his screaming face, digging into his neck, sucking fluids from him as his screams grow to an inhuman pitch.

"Let's get the fuck out of here!" Mitch cries.

January and Karl agree. They run for the exit, leaving Lyle and the police officer to the creatures. But when they open the apartment door, they find the hallway filled with more of the things. They squirm toward them the second they open the door, crawling across the walls and ceiling like grotesque spiders.

Mitch shuts the door and locks it.

"The bathroom," January yells.

They follow her toward the bathroom, jumping inside and shoving against the door. But one of the creatures catches them before they can shut it. It wraps its tentacles around Mitch's arm.

"It's got me!" Mitch cries, struggling against it.

Karl rushes to the door and slams it against the tentacle, but it doesn't let go. Mitch pulls off his leather jacket, revealing large blue welts forming on his arm where the tentacles are digging in.

January kicks the tentacle with the heel of her shoe until it releases Mitch, then they close the door and lock it. The creatures slam against the wood, curling their tentacles under the door. But it seems like it will hold.

"What the fuck was that?" January screams, pacing back and forth in the small bathroom.

Mitch moans, gripping his arm. His limb looks paralyzed. He can't move it. The thing just dangles loosely on his lap.

"What the fuck do we do?" Mitch cries. "They killed Lyle and that fucking cop! What the hell are they?"

January shakes her head. "I don't know."

Karl goes to the bathroom window and looks down into the street. There are hundreds of them out there, hissing and shrieking as they squirm up walls and down the sidewalks.

"They're everywhere," Karl says.

"What the fuck are we going to do?" Mitch asks.

January goes to Mitch and takes the tranquilizer gun from his limp arm. "We have to go to sleep. Pearson said that's the only way to escape them."

"Or we can just let them kill us," Karl says. "It's not like we can permanently die anymore."

January shakes her head. "I don't want to die that way. Do you?"

Karl shrugs.

When January checks Mitch's pockets for tranquilizer darts, she sees there are only two left. She loads the first one into the chamber and points it at Mitch.

"You're going first," she tells him.

Mitch nods his head, writhing in agony. "Please…"

She shoots him in the chest and he slowly loses consciousness. His cries go silent.

"So there's only one dart left," January says, holding out the pistol.

"You take it," Karl says. "I'll just kill myself."

"How?" January asks.

"Don't worry about it," he says. "I've killed myself thousands of times before. It won't be a problem."

She nods her head and points the gun at herself. The needle pierces her neck and she immediately drops to the ground from the pain. Her consciousness fades a few seconds later.

"Okay…" Karl says to himself. "It's just up to me now…"

He looks around the room, but doesn't see anything readily available for suicide. The creatures at the door seem

126

to now number in the dozens. Tentacles curl underneath the door, splitting apart the wood. Several more are now at the bathroom window, trying to break it. He has only seconds before they'll get to him.

Karl wonders why he's so terrified of the creatures. It's not like he fears death. He's killed himself so many times that death is no longer frightening. In fact, it's what he longs for more than anything. But for some reason, these creatures are different. He's desperate to get away from them, even if he has to kill himself to do it.

He goes under the bathroom sink and grabs some liquid plumber and downs whatever is left in the bottle. The burn in his throat makes him cough and gag, like acid is tearing apart his insides. But it doesn't kill him soon enough. He bangs his head onto the bathroom sink, trying to knock himself out. Blood sprays from his forehead. He becomes dizzy. He smashes his head one last time, using all of his strength, and feels his skull pop against the edge of the porcelain. Then he drops to the floor.

But he's not sure if it's enough. The bathroom door splits open and the creatures pour inside. His eyes roll back and his consciousness fades, as dozens of black shadows curl around his flesh and hiss into his ears.

CHAPTER
NINE

January wakes up in the morning, lying in her own bed. She jumps up, throwing the covers off of her, wondering what the hell just happened back there in the neverday. She gets to her feet and paces around the room, rubbing her skin. It's all still so fresh in her memory. What the hell were those things? Why did they attack them?

When she looks back at her bed, she almost didn't notice him before. Her boyfriend is lying there, fast asleep.

"Jason?" she asks.

She runs to him, wanting to get answers. He's explored the neverday before, so maybe he knows something she doesn't. She wonders if he's run into those creatures as well. She wonders if he knows what they are.

But when she pulls the covers off of him, she sees that Jason is dead, just as he was the last time she woke up next to him. He's lying in the same place, in the same position. His flesh is still covered in blue welts. His face still contorted in such a way that he had to have died in horrible pain.

"What the fuck is going on…" she says to him.

The corpse doesn't move.

The police don't show up at her door this morning. It's almost as though they know that Jason won't be waking up, like they know he's already dead.

January puts her shoes on, leaves the house and goes around the block to Karl's place. When she knocks on the door, there's no answer. At first, she wonders if Karl isn't awake yet. But that would be impossible. Karl always wakes up at least an hour before she does.

After a few more minutes, January loses patience. She breaks the window with a rock and crawls inside.

"Karl?" she calls out. "Are you in here?"

It's impossible, but for some reason she feels as though Karl is still back in the neverday, fighting off those creatures. She went to sleep before him, leaving him behind. For all she knows, he's still there, trying to survive. But she knows that's impossible. Even if he stayed in the neverday for several more weeks after her, he still would have woken up at the same time, in the same place, just like everyone else.

"Karl?" she calls out again.

As she says this, the bathroom door opens and Karl steps out, wrapped in a towel.

"Yeah?" he asks. When he sees her in his living room, shards of glass from his broken window scattered across the floor, he looks at her with a curious face. "What're you doing here?"

She holds her chest and sighs with relief. "I was worried something happened to you."

He shrugs, trying to keep his tiny towel from falling off his waist. "I just woke up here as usual. I took a longer shower than I normally do. Something about the neverday made me feel as if I haven't washed in ages."

"So you're okay?" she asks.

She goes to him and hugs him. She doesn't know why. She hardly even knows the guy. She's just thankful he's okay. But then she realizes his awkwardness as she's pressed against his wet body, wrapped only in a small towel. She lets him go and smiles, avoiding eye contact.

"I'm fine," Karl says, stepping back. "Let me get dressed and then we'll talk."

"It doesn't seem real," January says to Karl as they stroll through their suburban neighborhood toward the bus stop. "What the hell were those things?"

Karl shrugs.

"Do you think they're why we're repeating?" she asks.

"Maybe…" Karl says. "There's that theory that we repeat because the world is about to end. Remember, during orientation?"

January nods. "So you think the world ends because of a disease that turns everyone into those weird creatures?"

"People weren't transforming into those things. It was more like they were hosts to parasites that grew inside them."

"Like in the Alien movies?"

Karl shrugs like he doesn't know what she's talking about.

He says, "But if that is the way the world ends, what is causing us to repeat? Who has the ability to put us in an endless time loop?"

January shrugs. "Probably not humans. Aliens? Gods?"

"Whatever it is, I'm sure it's something we'll never understand."

January shakes her head. "But I won't accept that. I *have* to understand why it happens."

When they arrive at the bus stop, Karl looks back at her and says, "I don't care why. I just want it to stop."

"But if the time loop stopped, everyone would die."

Karl nods. "I would actually welcome that. I'm sick of immortality."

"Well, I don't want to die. I want my old life back."

Karl shakes his head. "That's not ever going to happen."

"If there's a way I want to find it."

Karl nods and looks away. He takes a deep breath of morning air.

"I hope you do," he says.

But the tone of his voice tells her that she doesn't have a chance in hell of accomplishing that.

When they get downtown to their group therapy, they look for the other people who went into the neverday with them. But the only person that has arrived is Tony. He sits in his chair, sweating more profusely than usual, shaking in his pants. Mitch and Lyle don't show.

The session has already started, so they are unable to speak to Tony until the break. While others share their problems, Tony just stares at them, freaking out over what happened. But January doesn't know why he's so nervous. He wasn't awake long enough to see what they had seen.

When they're let out, Tony leads the two of them down the hall to speak in private.

"What the hell happened?" he asks. "Did we get busted? Are the cops after us now?"

January shrugs. "I don't know. They didn't show up at my door this morning."

"I can't be on the run," Tony says. "I'm too hungover for that shit."

"Maybe we should start skipping our therapy sessions for a while," January says.

Karl shakes his head. "But that will only be more suspicious. Plus, I enjoy this group. I don't think we have anything to worry about if we play it cool."

Tony looks down the hall at the other people in their therapy group, making sure nobody's listening.

"So what happened?" he asks in a whispering tone.

January shakes her head. "You don't want to know."

"But what happened with the cop?" he asks. "Did you

get caught? He shot me with a dart or something."

Karl nods. "Yeah, he was trying to put us to sleep so we'd leave the neverday. But we took him down before he could get anyone else."

Tony takes a deep breath, somewhat relieved by these words.

"So how much later did you stay awake after that?" he asks. "Did you learn anything else?"

January and Karl look at each other, wondering if they should tell the whole story. January shakes her head, trying to convince him with her eyes not to say anything.

But Karl tells him anyway. "You killed Lyle."

"What?" Tony yells, so loud that people look in their direction. He lowers his voice. "What do you mean I killed him?"

Karl thinks about it. "Well, it wasn't you exactly. Something came out of you."

"What the hell came out of me?"

"There were things that came out of everyone who was asleep. They attacked us. Lyle and the cop were killed. I had to commit suicide in order to escape."

Tony presses his hands to his head, not able to wrap his mind around the new information.

Karl smiles. "Yeah, it was pretty fucked up."

"But…" Tony says. "Why did something come out of me?"

January explains. "The disease that put everyone in comas. It was caused by some kind of parasitic life form that was growing inside of them. At least, that's what it seemed like to me."

"So what are we going to do?" Tony asks.

January shrugs. "I still want answers."

"Should we stay awake again tonight?" Karl asks. "Maybe we'll learn more about why it happens."

Tony shakes his head. "Fuck that. I'm not entering the neverday ever again."

January agrees with the fat guy. "Yeah, I don't think we're ready for that yet. We need to find the others. There's also the police officer we talked to. He obviously knows a lot more about this than we do. We have to talk to him."

"No fucking way," Tony says. "We need to stay far away from the police. You're still new. You don't know what they're like."

"He hasn't turned us in yet," January says. "Perhaps we can reason with him."

Karl nods his head in agreement. "Let's do it."

"I'm out," Tony says, stepping away from them.

"He'll remember us no matter what," January says. "The only way to get out of this is to convince him not to turn us in."

But Tony doesn't listen.

"Pretend we never even met," he says.

Then he rushes down the hall to the elevator. He doesn't go back to the session. He just runs away, too frightened to deal with the situation.

Karl tries to go after him, but January grabs him by the arm.

"Let him go," she says. "He's useless to us now."

Karl nods in agreement, watching Tony as he disappears into the elevator.

Then January tells him, "We'll just do as he says and pretend we never met him. If we do get into trouble we don't need to bring him down with us."

January and Karl go back to group. They sit through the session, wondering what their next move should be.

In the last half hour, they see a familiar face. Mitch walks through the door, interrupting the session. He looks as panicked as Tony when he enters. He locks eyes with January and Karl, like he wants to speak to them immediately.

"Mr. Murphy…" Nick addresses the latecomer. "Glad to see you finally made it."

Mitch nods. "Sorry. I had some trouble getting here."

Mitch takes the seat that Tony left empty. As he crosses the circle, January notices something off about him. He's clutching his arm, the same arm that was wounded by the creatures in the neverday.

Nick smiles at the latecomer, keeping his eyes on him. "Well, since you've captured all of our attentions coming in this late, perhaps you should go next. We haven't heard from you yet."

Mitch has a terrified look on his face. He glances to January and then back to Nick. "No, thank you. I'd prefer not to. I'm not feeling good today."

But Nick doesn't let him slide. "I insist. You look troubled. Please tell us about it."

Mitch doesn't seem to know how to get out of talking. He looks at the door as though wondering if he should just run away. But then he gives in and nods his head.

"So, yeah…" Mitch says. "I'm Mitch Murphy. I've been repeating for… I don't know. Less than a week, I guess."

As he speaks, he clutches his arm tightly through his leather jacket. He's obviously in intense pain.

"My main problem is that I…" He pauses to wince. "I don't live here. I wake up in a van passing through town… my band was on tour… so I don't really have a home… My family is on the east coast… I don't know if I'll ever see them again…"

January and Karl look at each other. They're both worried about their friend. His pain only seems to intensify by the minute. The others in the room notice it as well. They all stare at him intensely, more concerned by his cringing facial expressions than the words he's saying.

When Mitch notices how he's coming across, he tries to compose himself.

"I don't know if my parents are repeating," he says. "I haven't tried emailing them yet. But if they are I hope I can get a plane ticket to see them, even if it's just for a few hours."

Even though he's trying to hide his pain, he still can't cover it up completely.

After he takes a pause to cringe and grip his arm, Nick asks, "Are you okay? You look like you're hurt…"

Mitch shakes his head. "It's nothing."

Nick won't accept that. "No, you look like you're dying over there. What's the matter?"

Mitch tries to brush it off. "I had a bad fall on the

way over and hurt my arm pretty bad."

Nick nods his head and gets to his feet. "Let me look at it…"

Mitch shakes his head. "No, it's no big deal."

"It could be dislocated," Nick says. "Let me check it out. I might be able to help."

Mitch jumps back as Nick approaches him, but then goes into a serious fit of pain. He drops from his chair and writhes on the ground, screaming and clutching at his arm. Everyone stands up from their chairs and stares at him, wondering what's going on.

"Get away from me," Mitch yells.

But he's too weak to resist as Nick pulls up the sleeve on his leather jacket, revealing the wounds on Mitch's arm.

When January sees them, her eyes widen. Mitch's arm is covered in blue welts, the same wounds he received while they were in the neverday. They didn't go away after he went to sleep. Not only that, but they seem even worse than before. His flesh is swollen, infected. Something is pulsing under his skin.

"Have you been in the neverday?" Nick asks as he examines the strange wounds, his eyebrows curling in disgust.

Then Nick jumps away from Mitch and pulls out a walkie-talkie from his belt loop. He puts his mouth to it and yells, "Code red! Code red! Room 1803!"

Everyone in the room looks at each other in confusion as he says this, looking at each other and wondering what's going on.

"Get out, everyone!" Nick yells at the group. "Stay away from him!"

The group is in shock, but they do as he says. Everyone rushes out of the room quicker than if it was full of tear gas.

January and Karl are resistant at first. They stare down at Mitch's writhing body, wondering what is happening to him. He looks at them with fear in his eyes. But there's nothing they can do.

As they leave the room, five security officers rush inside, nearly knocking them both down. They turn back and watch through the window as the security guards cover Mitch's face in a black hood and handcuff his hands behind his back, making sure not to touch the pulsing wounds on his arm.

"Let's get the fuck out of here," January says.

Karl agrees.

They run for the elevator, passing the confused people standing in the hallway. Not a single one of them seem to know what's going on.

January and Karl are so terrified of what just happened that they don't want to talk about it. Instead, they focus on finding the last person in their group: Lyle Conway. They look up his address online and take the bus to his apartment across the river.

But when they knock on his door, there's no answer.

"Hey Lyle, are you awake?" January says through the door.

But there's only silence on the other side.

"Let's break it down," Karl says.

January shakes her head. "That will draw too much attention. Let's go through a window." She points at the half-open kitchen window over the railing.

Karl nods his head.

It's lucky he lives on the ground floor or else they wouldn't have been able to reach it. They go through the grass, behind some bushes, and pry off the screen.

"Are you sure nobody's going to notice?" Karl asks, looking around at all the apartment windows around them.

"Everyone's at work," she says, pointing at all the empty parking spots. "Don't worry about it."

The two of them crawl through the narrow window, rolling over a pile of dirty dishes stacked in the kitchen sink.

"Lyle?" January calls out when she gets back on her feet.

There's still no reply. They go through his grubby apartment, heading for the bedroom. But the bed is empty.

"Where is he?" she asks.

Karl shrugs. He's not in the bathroom or living room. The whole apartment is empty.

"Do you think he left?" January asks.

"He might not have slept at his own place," Karl says. "We don't know where he wakes up each rotation. He could have been sleeping at a girlfriend's place or something."

January shakes her head. "There's no way that guy has a girlfriend."

"How do you know?"

January shrugs. "He's got that lonely single guy look about him. If he's not here then he must have left. Maybe he's on the run."

Karl pulls back a curtain and looks out the sliding glass door. He turns back to January and says, "No, he's out here."

They step out on the balcony and find Lyle asleep at a table. He's got a makeshift desk out there. His head lies on an open laptop.

"He must have passed out while writing before the time loop," Karl says.

January doesn't respond. She approaches the writer, calling out to him. "Lyle? Are you awake?"

But when she goes around the table to him, she sees that he's not moving. His body is covered in blue welts. His eyes are wide open, a look of horror frozen on his face.

She jumps back and cries, "Oh, fuck…"

"What?" Karl asks, going in to see for himself.

"He's dead," she says.

Karl feels for a pulse and then closes his eyes. "What happened to him?"

January shakes her head, not able to believe it. "He's just like Jason, my boyfriend." She looks closer. "He has the same blue welts on his skin. They died the same way."

Karl points at them. "Those are the same marks that Mitch had on his arms. The creatures did this."

"But the day has restarted," she says. "The wounds wouldn't still be there."

Karl shakes his head. "But Mitch's wounds didn't

disappear. It's like the creatures can attack us outside of the time loop."

"So Jason is permanently dead…" January says.

Karl nods. "If he was attacked by the creatures I think there's a good chance that he is. Lyle as well."

"But how…" January says.

"Call the cop," Karl says. "Officer Pearson. He died in the neverday as well. If he's the same as Lyle and your boyfriend then we'll know it's true."

January agrees. She calls the police department and asks for Paul Pearson. They tell her that he hasn't come into work that day. The person on the other line seems upset about it. She says that he's taking a sick day, but January can tell something isn't right about the excuse. When she asks about when he'll be back into work, she isn't given an exact answer. She's pretty sure that he'll never be into work again.

When January hangs up, she shakes her head at Karl.

"He's dead," she says. "He has to be."

Karl nods and turns away. Both of them feel guilty for his death. They tied him to the chair. They're the ones who got him killed.

"So what do we do now?" Karl asks.

"We need more answers," she says. "We need to talk to other people who have been in the neverday."

"Like Dwayne?" Karl asks.

January nods her head. "Yeah, he might know more than he let on. We should talk to him next."

They go after Dwayne at his work. All they knew about the man, outside of being an ex-con who used to explore the neverday, was that he bagged groceries for a living. They hit seven stores in the downtown area before they come across the one Dwayne works at.

When he sees them, Dwayne pretends he doesn't know who they are. He was there in group when Mitch was attacked by security guards. He knows they've all been in the neverday. He doesn't want anything to do with them.

Karl and January hang out in the store for a couple of hours, trying to get his attention. They know he won't talk while working, so they wait for him to go on break. They follow him out back to the employee smoking area. Dwayne just shakes his head at them as they approach.

"You two better stay the fuck away from me," he tells them. "I don't want anyone thinking we're friends."

January says, "Just answer our questions and we'll never talk to you again."

Dwayne looks at both of them, staring them both down. After a moment of silence, he gives in by letting out a sigh.

"You have until the end of our smokes," he says, holding out his pack of cigarettes. "But if anyone comes by, pretend we don't know each other. We're just smoking strangers hanging out by a butt can."

January agrees. She takes a cigarette and lights up. Karl takes one as well, but he doesn't smoke it. He just lets it burn in his hand.

"I saw what happened to Mitch," Dwayne says, not looking them in the eyes as he speaks to them. "You guys went that deep on your first trip?"

January nods. "Yeah, we wanted to stay up for as long as we could."

"Stupid…" Dwayne says, shaking his head.

"So you know about the creatures?" Karl asks.

Dwayne looks at them. "You could say that."

"What are they?" January asks.

Dwayne shrugs. "Pure fucking evil. That's all I know. I used to meet a group of people there. We didn't know each other outside of the neverday. It was a rule that we didn't interact with each other in normal time. It's safer that way, harder for the cops to trace those they catch back to the rest of us." He takes a long drag on his cigarette. "Anyway, we were determined to figure out what the hell was going on. We used to meet at a house in Southeast and board the place up so the creatures couldn't get in. We'd watch them for days. At first, we thought they were just some kind of alien parasitic beings that incubated in human hosts. But the more we watched them, the less this seemed to be true. The creatures didn't eat or sleep. They didn't interact with each other. They seemed to have only one purpose and that was to kill any human who was still awake in the neverday."

"So you don't think they're alien?" January asks.

Dwayne shakes his head. "I think they're demonic. I think what happens in the neverday is book of revelation hell on earth shit. And the reason we repeat is the result of divine intervention. It's all just God taking pity on us, trying to save us from damnation."

"You actually believe that?" January asks.

Dwayne nods. "Hell yeah I do. If you've seen all that I've seen, you would too."

"What happened to the other people you knew in the neverday?"

"Dead," Dwayne says. "The creatures got most of them. The others were caught by the police and had their brains scrambled. The only person I know who might still be going in the neverday is a guy named Jason Rogers."

January's eyes light up when he says that name.

"The two of us were the last from our group," Dwayne continues. "When I gave up, he said he was determined to keep going with or without me. I told him to fuck off and never spoke to him again. If you want more answers, he's the one you have to talk to. It's been several months since I've seen him last. There's a chance he's learned more about the creatures during this time."

January shakes her head at him. "Jason's already dead."

"You know him?" Dwayne asks.

January nods. "He was my boyfriend. For the past two mornings, I've woken up with his dead body next to mine. He's covered in the same blue welts that were on Mitch's arm."

When Dwayne hears this, it hits him hard. He looks down, holding back tears. January realizes they must have been a lot closer than he let on. Even she wasn't so broken up over his death.

"Fuck…" Dwayne says, rubbing his eyes. "I always

hoped he would make it. I'm sorry…"

January takes a puff of her cigarette. She lets the guy stand there in silence for a few minutes, not wanting to have to console him over her own boyfriend's death.

"So is there anyone else we could talk to?" she asks. "Did he have any other friends who might have started going into the neverday with him after you left?"

Dwayne shakes his head. "I don't know. It was just us. I haven't been in communication with him since I started repeating normally again."

"Are you sure there's nobody else?" January asks.

Karl asks, "Maybe somebody else you met while exploring the neverday?"

Dwayne shakes his head at them, but then he pauses and thinks about it.

"Well, actually…" He looks around to make sure nobody's looking. "There was another group that was in the neverday with us, but you don't want to go anywhere near them."

"Who?" January asks.

"They're with the government," Dwayne says. "Well, the *new* government. They have a facility they operate out of. It's impenetrable, to both people and those creatures. I'm sure they know far more than we ever learned about what's happening in the neverday. But you'll want to stay far away from them. They're the ones that scramble your brains if they find out you've been in the neverday."

January's eyes widen at the thought. She doesn't care about the danger, if there are people who know more about what's happening in the neverday she wants to find them.

"Where's this facility?" she asks.

Dwayne shakes his head. "I never should have mentioned it. You don't want to go there."

But she insists. "It doesn't matter how dangerous it is. If they have answers I want to find them."

"I'm not telling you," he says. "I should have stopped you from going into the neverday in the first place. You're going to get yourself killed."

"So what?" she says. "If we get killed then you don't have to worry about us anymore. Just tell us."

Dwayne sighs. "The man you want to find is named Michael Stockman. He's the one who's been repeating longer than anyone else in town. He's supposed to be hundreds of years old."

"I've heard of him," January says.

"He's supposed to be the one in charge," Dwayne says. "The facility is on a hill by OHSU. The medical college. Don't try going there during the neverday. It'll be locked tight." He finishes his cigarette and tosses it into a coffee can ashtray. "That's all I can tell you. I've never gotten in before. Only an idiot would try."

January nods. She looks at Karl. "We'll try there next."

As they walk away, Dwayne says, "Don't say I didn't warn you."

But January just waves him off as they walk away. She's determined to learn all she can about what's happening, no matter what the cost.

"Are you with me?" she asks Karl, as they leave the back of the grocery store toward the parking lot.

Karl nods. "Yeah, let's do it."

"I'm seeing this through to the end," she tells him. "Even if this Michael Stockman person won't help us, I won't give up until I have all the answers."

CHAPTER
TEN

Karl Lybeck is having the time of his life. Every day seems to be more exciting than the last. He hopes it never ends. He can tell that January is worried about dying, despite all of her determination. But the fact that dying is a possibility is what excites Karl more than anything. He's lived for so long without the possibility of death that he knows how boring life can be without it. He likes that there could be consequences for his actions. He likes that his odds of survival are not very high. Because even if he dies in the end, the whole experience will be worthwhile. For him, death is a reward in itself.

They take a cab to OHSU and climb the hill up to the facility Dwayne had told them about.

"So do you know what we're going to say to them once we get there?" Karl asks.

January shrugs. "We're not going to talk to them at all. We're breaking in."

When she says this, a smile brightens on Karl's face. "Yes, let's do that. It'll be more fun."

But when they get to the facility, the place is like a fortress. There are no windows. A tall fence covered in razor wire surrounds the building. The only entrance is heavily guarded by men in black uniforms, carrying machine guns.

They hide in the bushes and examine the place from a distance.

"That's not going to be easy to break into," Karl says, trying to hold back his excitement.

January sighs. "We have to sneak in another way."

"Maybe there's a secret underground entrance," Karl says.

January shakes her head. "That would take too much time. If we had days we might be able to figure it out but we've got to get in there tonight. There's a good chance Mitch told the cops about us. If he did, then they know where we live. They'll catch us when we wake up in the morning."

"So what should we do?"

January points at the trucks driving into the facility. They are carrying supplies, probably everything they'll need for exploring the neverday for long periods of time.

"We get on one of those trucks," she says.

"And then what?" Karl asks.

She shrugs. "We'll have to improvise once we get in, but we need to find Michael Stockman. He's the one who will have the information we're looking for."

"Won't he turn us in?" Karl asks. "Even if we tie him up in a closet somewhere and get all the information we need, he'll remember our faces. He'll have the police after us in the morning."

January shakes her head. "I don't care. I've got to know."

Karl nods and says, "Sure. I'll follow your lead."

But he wonders if she's okay. She seems to be acting kind of crazy ever since they left the neverday. She seems reckless and desperate. He knows that she'll probably get them both killed, but he's fine with that. He'd rather be reckless than play it safe. He's lived too long to bother with playing it safe.

They both know it's a stupid plan, but they try it anyway.

When the next truck comes down the road leading to the facility, they jump out of the bushes and run behind it, trying to stay clear of the driver's rearview mirror. But when they get to the back of the vehicle, they can't get the door open. January jumps up onto the back of the truck, fidgeting with the handle, trying to pull it up. Karl is a little slower and can barely keep up with the truck even at its speed of 20 miles per hour.

The truck slows to a stop and waits as the security guards open the gate. Karl uses the opportunity to get on the back of the vehicle next to January, trying to help her get the door open.

"It's locked," she says.

Karl looks at her struggling with the handle. "Are you serious?"

"Forget it," she says. "We should run for it."

But before they can jump off, the truck pulls forward,

driving them through the gate toward the facility.

The security doesn't notice them hanging on the back of the truck as they're driven through the yard toward the entrance. When the vehicle comes to a stop, they have no idea what to do. The front gate closes and they find themselves trapped in the yard with nowhere to run. They look around. The ground is all asphalt with no bushes or dumpsters they can hide behind.

"Under the truck," January whispers.

Karl follows her. They get down on their bellies and wiggle their way beneath the vehicle just before the driver comes around the side to open the back door.

"This isn't going to work," January says.

Karl shrugs. It was her idea. He's just following her lead.

When the facility doors open, two men step out and help the driver unload supplies into the building.

"We have to crawl inside when they're not looking," Karl whispers to her, pointing at the entrance.

January nods. She breathes heavily, making so much noise that Karl's surprised the men haven't heard her already.

They wait for several minutes, watching steel-toed boots stepping back and forth from the vehicle. There's no way they can sneak around them. They'd be found the second they crawled out from under the truck.

"What do we do?" January asks.

"Be patient," Karl whispers.

January examines the bottom of the vehicle.

"Maybe we can ride this truck out of here if we find

a way to hold on," she says, looking for handholds.

Karl shakes his head. "Only if we have to. There still might be a way in."

The three men never leave the truck's side, even after they finish unloading it.

"You got a cigarette?" one of them asks another.

"Sure…"

Two of the men light cigarettes and lean against the side of the truck, smoking casually. It seems everyone smokes in this world now. Since lung cancer isn't an issue, there must not be as many regulations as there used to be.

"It's so fucking hot…" one of the men complains. "I'll never get used to this weather."

The other one says. "What are you talking about? The weather's perfect."

"It's too warm for me. I wish it was cooler."

"For having to repeat the same day over and over again, this is a good day for it. I couldn't imagine what it would be like if we were repeating in the winter."

January and Karl look at each other, listening to the conversation. They wonder if they're distracted enough to make a break for it.

"Oh, I *wish* it was winter," one of the men says. "I love the cold weather. Give me gray skies and cool winds over sunny, sweaty heat any day."

The other man snorts and says, "You're crazy. It would be a living hell if we were repeating in the winter. All those people with seasonal affective disorder? People would be even more depressed than they already are."

"But I have reverse seasonal affective disorder. I get depressed in the summer."

"Nobody gets depressed in the summer."

"Well, *I* do. I hate summer."

"It's only April. You're lucky we're not repeating on an *actual* hot day."

"Yeah, but this weather feels as bad as summer. It's a good thing it cools down at night or I would've gone insane by now."

As the men get deeper into the conversation, January decides to make her move. Karl follows her as she crawls to the side of the truck closest to the entrance.

She looks back at Karl. He nods at her.

Then they both run for it.

"You should go up to Mt. Hood someday," one of the men says. "It's still cold up there at this time of year."

Karl looks back at the men for a second as they enter the building. They're too involved in conversation to notice him.

"Yeah, if I can ever get off work," the other man says. "They haven't given me a day off in months."

"It pays good, though…"

Karl doesn't hear the rest of the conversation as he sneaks inside, following January. He closes the door behind him as quietly as he can and it locks electronically. If the two men don't have key cards they won't be able to get inside. Karl knows it might cause a fuss if the two are locked out, but they'll surely believe it closed by accident. At least they won't come in behind them and catch them by surprise.

Karl and January find themselves in a hallway with a tall ceiling. The walls are lined with boxes and crates filled with supplies. There's only a small path through the center that they can squeeze through.

"Keep going," January tells him, as she walks casually through the stocks of boxes.

When they get through, they run into the third man who unloaded the truck. He is busy bringing the boxes into a side storeroom.

When he sees January, he just says, "Hey, how's it going?"

And then goes back to work, like he assumes she's supposed to be there.

January nods back at him and continues down the hallway. Karl follows after her.

When they're far enough away from the guy, she whispers at Karl, "I guess if all else fails, just act like you belong here. It's always a better option than panicking and running away."

"But it won't work with everyone," Karl says.

January nods. "Probably not."

They avoid the elevator and go to the stairwell, knowing that most people avoid taking stairs—especially in a world where physical fitness doesn't matter anymore.

The place isn't that tall. Only three or four stories. They decide to go all the way to the top.

"How are we supposed to recognize Michael Stockman?" Karl asks.

January shrugs. "Maybe he has an office with his name on it?"

Karl shakes his head. "I doubt he worked here before the rotation. He's only in charge because he's been awake the longest."

"Then we have to ask somebody," she says. "We'll jump the first person we see."

Karl nods. But then thinks about it and says, "Maybe we should have jumped the guy downstairs."

January shakes her head. "It would have been too risky. Security is tightest near the entrance. Besides, the guy didn't seem like he knew anything. We need somebody on a top floor."

When they get upstairs to the entrance to the fourth floor, they can't get the door open. Unlike the doors on the lower levels, this one is electronically locked and requires a key card.

"This has got to be it," January says.

"But how do we get in?"

January shrugs.

"Should we go to a lower level and see if we can get up from there?" Karl asks.

"No, I doubt it would be any easier. We have to wait until somebody opens the door."

"But how long will that take?"

January shrugs. "Hopefully not long."

They wait on the other side of the door for an hour, ready to jump whoever comes through it. But nobody ever does. They wait there all day, not sure what to do. Night falls. They hear noises on the other side, people talking and walking around. Whoever is behind it, they are very busy making preparations for whatever they're planning to do during the neverday.

"We won't be able to leave if we wait any longer," Karl says. "It'll be the neverday soon."

January nods. "Maybe that's for the best."

"What do you mean?" Karl asks.

"I doubt everyone working here will stay awake during the neverday. There will be fewer people to worry about."

"But how the hell are we going to stay awake that long? We don't have cocaine or anything."

January looks down at the stairs.

"Exercise could keep us awake," she says. "We can just climb up and down them whenever we're tired."

Karl shakes his head. "That's going to wear us out eventually. It'll only make us more tired."

"If we keep our heart rates up we'll stay awake."

"Not if our muscles stop working."

They try to stay awake for as long as they can, even trying to use the stairs whenever they're tired. But they don't make it very far into the neverday before they're ready to fall asleep.

"What time is it?" Karl asks.

January looks at her phone. "Five in the morning."

"We need to act before we pass out," Karl says.

"But it's not really the neverday yet."

Karl shrugs. "Anyone who's going to sleep during the neverday probably already went home by now."

She nods and gets to her feet. "Okay, let's do it."

"Do what?" Karl asks.

January points at the door. "I'm going to knock until somebody answers. We'll jump whoever opens the door, pull them into the hallway and ask them some questions. Then knock them out so they don't tell anyone we're here."

"Sounds like you've got it all figured out," Karl says.

January shrugs. "It's all I've got."

The two of them wait at the door, preparing themselves to grab whoever steps through. January looks back at Karl, holding up her fist and aiming it at the door.

Before she does it, Karl says, "Do a causal, friendly knock. Something musical. They'll expect you're just a part of the staff if you do that. A loud, frantic knock might put them on alert."

January nods. She knocks five times on the door in a musical rhythm just as Karl suggested. It's the kind of friendly knock that you'd never expect to hear from a stranger.

But nobody comes.

January knocks again in a different yet no less friendly pattern.

Still, nobody comes.

"Fuck…" January says. "Now what?"

Karl shrugs. "Maybe they're too busy to hear."

January knocks again. Then she presses her ear to the door. There's no sound coming from the other side anymore.

"Shit…" she says.

As she waits for somebody who doesn't answer, a horrifying thought crosses her mind.

"What if we got the wrong place?" she asks.

Karl looks up at her with a questioning face.

She explains, "What if Dwayne was wrong and they aren't actually exploring the neverday here? It could just be some normal business. What if we're trapped here until the creatures come out?"

Karl shakes his head. "It has to be the right place. Besides, we still have plenty of time before the creatures come out. We can go to sleep whenever we want."

January knocks on the door again, this time hard and furiously.

"Calm down," Karl says. "Stick to the plan. They'll come eventually."

But January doesn't listen to him. She bangs on the door as loudly as she can, yelling for somebody to answer.

When the door opens, January and Karl are caught off guard. They're not ready to jump the person who answers. And, even if they were, they wouldn't have stood a chance.

A large man appears in the doorway. He's twice the size of Karl and January put together. A tall, muscled man with thick glasses, a scruffy black beard, and a white polo shirt tucked into khaki pants. He's the biggest, toughest nerd either of them has ever seen in their lives.

The man smiles at them and says, "We were wondering when you were going to come in."

Karl and January look at each other, confused by the massive man's friendly disposition.

"We've been watching you all night," he says. Then he points at a lens on the ceiling, next to the light. "You've been on camera this whole time."

"Seriously?" January asks him. "Why didn't you come after us?"

The man shrugs. "You weren't doing any harm." Then he widens the door and gestures for them to enter. "Come in. I'll make you some coffee."

Karl and January look at each other again, not sure what to make of him. But they decide to accept his offer.

They step into a hallway filled with offices and laboratories. He leads them into some kind of small break room with a kitchen counter, refrigerator and a single round table surrounded by metal chairs.

Another man sits at the table, typing on a laptop. He's the polar opposite of the large man—a short, skinny young man with prominent cheekbones and a shaved head. When he sees them enter, he smiles in delight at the sight of Karl and January.

"You let them in?" the skinny man asks, pleasantly surprised.

The large man nods. "Well, I couldn't leave them out there all morning. That would be rude."

The skinny man smiles and nods, and then goes back to his laptop.

"My name's Ridge," says the large man. "This is Patrick. We work the *long hours* together."

"The long hours?" January asks.

"That's what we call the neverday here," he explains. Then he goes to the coffee machine and starts a new pot.

"So it's true?" January asks. "You really do study the neverday here?"

He nods. "Of course."

"And you don't care that we know?"

He shrugs. "It's not exactly a secret. We have a website and everything."

Patrick nods. "It's what I'm working on now."

"So you're not going to scramble our brains?" January asks.

Ridge lets out a deep chuckle. "You're thinking of the cops. We don't do that here."

January sighs with relief and sits down in a chair across from Patrick. "I was worried there for a minute…"

"Oh, I'm sorry…" Ridge begins. "We probably will have to turn you over to the cops. I just meant that *we* wouldn't scramble your brains."

January's eyes widen after he says this.

"Oh…" she says.

Ridge shrugs as he pours two cups of coffee. "But don't worry about it too much. They don't do that to everyone they catch in the neverday. They just do it to the unruly types. The people who are insistent on telling the world about what they discover."

He hands January a cup of coffee. "You're not the unruly type, are you?"

January shrugs. She holds the coffee cup up to her mouth and takes a sip.

"Of course you're not," Ridge says. "If you were we wouldn't be able to have a cup of coffee together. You'd be demanding answers and causing a fuss. We can reason with a person like you."

January nods. She looks at Karl, who just smiles back at her.

"Thank you," Karl says to Ridge as he hands him the other cup of coffee.

"See?" Ridge says, pointing at Karl. "You're both civilized people. I'm sure you'll be fine."

The large man pours himself a cup of coffee and sits them down at the table next to his coworker.

"So what brought the two of you here?" he asks.

"We wanted to talk to Michael Stockman," January says. "We thought he'd have answers about what happens in the neverday."

Ridge smiles and nods. "I see. So what exactly do you know about the neverday so far?"

"We stayed awake for over six days," she says.

Ridge sighs and nods his head. "That's very dangerous. You shouldn't have done that."

"We lost a friend," she says. "Another was injured. The police took him away this morning."

Ridge's thick lips curl up as he listens intently, nodding at each sentence.

"It's really a shame," he says. "The long hours shouldn't be explored haphazardly."

"What are those creatures anyway?" January asks. "Where do they come from?"

Ridge shakes his head. "I'm not at liberty to say. That would be up to Michael."

"Can we speak to him?" Karl asks.

Ridge looks over at him and says, "I can ask. But there are no guarantees. He's a very busy man."

"We would appreciate it if you'd try," January says.

Ridge nods and stands out of his seat. "I'll see what he's up to, but he's usually busy making preparations at this time."

"Thank you," Karl says, smiling at the large man.

Ridge bows at him and goes toward the doorway. He turns briefly to say, "Enjoy your coffee."

And then leaves the room, closing the door behind him.

Karl and January sit at the table with the petite, bald man on the laptop, sipping their coffees and staring at the back of his computer.

"So what do you put on your website?" January asks him.

Patrick shrugs. "I'm just a programmer. I don't actually post anything."

"What's the site for?"

He shrugs again.

"We use it to communicate with other groups in the long hours," he says. "There are facilities like this one all over the world. We're not the largest, but we're among the first."

"How long have you been working here?"

"Not very long. Only about twenty years or so."

"That's not long?" January asks.

He shrugs. "Ridge has been here a couple hundred years. There are people who have been here even longer."

"Doesn't it get boring?" Karl asks.

Patrick smiles. "No way. I love this job. I could do it forever." He looks down at his keyboard and pauses to type in some code. "I probably will be."

Before January can ask another question, the door to the break room opens. Ridge is standing in the doorway, talking to somebody in the hall.

"It won't take long," Ridge says.

"I don't have time right now," says the voice in the hallway. "Get rid of them."

"But we can use them," Ridge says. "Without Lange and Trevors, we're short-staffed this rotation."

"New people will only hold us back," says the man in the hall.

"They'll catch on quickly. I'm sure of it."

"They're a security risk."

"At least come in and meet them," Ridge says, pushing the door open wider.

Karl and January see a man with long blond hair and wire-framed glasses standing in the hall. Even though his body appears to be in his mid to late thirties, his eyes look much older. He's obviously been alive for a very long time. Karl recognizes the age in his eyes. He sees it in himself whenever he looks in the mirror each morning.

The man in the hallway lets out a sigh and says, "I don't have time. If you think you can use them then do with them what you want. But they're your responsibility. Leave me out of it."

But as the man says this, he takes a peek into the room. When he sees Karl and January, he pauses. He squints his eyes in their direction.

"Is that…" he says, adjusting his glasses.

Ridge smiles and leads the man into the room.

"I'd like to introduce you to Michael Stockman," Ridge says to Karl and January.

But Michael Stockman doesn't enter. His mouth widens. He can't take his eyes off of the intruders.

"Karl?" asks Michael Stockman, his voice confused and full of disbelief. "Karl Lybeck?"

Karl looks up at him, wondering why he knows his name.

"Is that really you?" Stockman asks.

Karl nods. "Yes, I'm Karl Lybeck."

Stockman smiles and rushes into the room. He stops right in front of Karl and examines him, looking him up and down. Everyone else is confused by his reaction, especially Karl. Patrick looks up from his laptop. January misses her mouth when she tries to take a sip of coffee.

"You know each other?" Ridge asks.

Stockman nods. "Yeah… from a very long time ago."

Ridge scratches his beard. "Did he work for you or something?"

"No…" Stockman shakes his head. "He didn't work for me. *I* used to work for *him*." He turns to Ridge. "He's the man responsible for this. *All* of this. If it wasn't for Karl Lybeck none of us would even be here."

CHAPTER
ELEVEN

January has a hard time understanding what's going on. She knew Karl claimed to have been awake for thousands of years, but he always seemed just as clueless about the new world as she was. She watches Stockman wrap his arms around Karl and hug him as tightly as he would a long lost brother.

"I can't believe you're finally back," Stockman says. "After all these years… I never thought I'd see you again."

Karl pulls himself out of the man's embrace and says, "I'm sorry, but I don't know who you are. You're saying we've met before?"

When Stockman looks into Karl's eyes, he lets out a sigh and says, "So it worked. You really were able to forget it all…"

Karl shrugs. "I don't know what you mean."

Stockman goes to the coffee machine and pours himself a cup. Then he turns back to Karl.

"Several hundred years ago, you told me you wanted to retire," he says. "Our work had taken its toll on you.

You said you wanted to forget it all and give up."

Karl shakes his head. "I've forgotten most of my past, but I don't remember ever meeting anyone else who was awake. It was always just me. I've been killing myself every day for as long as I can remember."

Stockman nods his head. "Yes, you said that's what you would do. You must have been killing yourself for so long that you've forgotten everything. Just as you hoped you would."

"But I don't understand…" Karl says. "How could I forget knowing about other people in my situation? I've longed for some kind of change in my life for as long as I can remember. If I knew there was a society of people living as I was, I would never have given up on life."

"I'm not sure what you've been through since we spoke last," Stockman says. "I know that you were around for centuries before I woke up. You taught me how to live in this world. We were like brothers for hundreds of years. And when others started waking up, we built a community together."

Karl pauses, thinking about what he's saying, but then he shakes his head. He doesn't remember anything.

"I don't know…" he says. "It's not coming back to me."

But as Karl seems distressed and confused over the situation, January couldn't be happier about it. She broke into the place in order to get information out of Michael Stockman, and now that it turns out that he's an old friend of Karl's then he'll surely be able to help them.

She takes the opportunity to confront him.

"So can you tell us everything you know about the

neverday?" January asks. "We came here for answers."

Stockman looks over at January, just realizing her for the first time.

He nods his head at her. "Of course. I'll tell you everything." Then he looks back at Karl. "Come with me. There's been so much progress since you left. I must tell you all about it."

Karl takes his hand and stands up.

"Okay, but you'll have to start at the beginning," Karl says. "I don't remember any of it."

Stockman takes Karl and January on a tour of the facility, going through the different labs and offices, showing them everything they could ever possibly want to see and more.

"There's only seventeen of us now," Stockman says. "That number has changed dramatically throughout the years. There was a time when it was only two or three of us. Other times we've had up to sixty people on staff. Twenty-two is the magic number, though. We like to have twenty-two people working here at all times."

"What do they all do?" January asks, examining the busy people they pass at the various work stations in the building.

Stockman replies, "Surveillance, research, and communications are our three main departments. We mostly study the long hours and try not to get ourselves killed."

"How long do you stay in the neverday?" Karl asks.

"We've gotten it up to five months per rotation," Stockman says.

January's mouth drops in disbelief. "Seriously? That long? How do you do it?"

"We sleep," Stockman says, bringing them to a few small offices that have been transformed into makeshift bunk rooms. Four bunks per office.

"What do you mean you sleep?" January asks.

"We've developed a drug that we manufacture here that prevents REM sleep." Stockman brings them to a chemistry lab where three women are mixing chemicals and white powders. "You won't restart if you never fall into a deep enough sleep. It's much more effective than stimulants, but it takes its toll on you eventually. We've found that a hundred and fifty days is the limit for most people. Your memory becomes unreliable after that."

"So you're only on day one of a hundred and fifty?" January asks. "You plan to go that far into the neverday?"

Stockman nods. "Ridge, the large man you've already met, has been able to go for years into the long hours. He's made of stronger stuff than the rest of us. But because he's the only one, there's not much he's able to do on his own. Three years has been his limit. But the Paris team has gone even longer."

"And the creatures can't break in here during that time?" January asks.

He shakes his head. "Nothing gets in or out. They could probably get in if they knew we were here, but this building is high on a hill away from the rest of the city, there are no windows, no sound escapes these walls. As long as we don't leave, we're perfectly safe."

"How do you study them if you never leave?" January asks.

"We have cameras set up all over town and can observe everything from here," he says. "And we also keep a few specimens downstairs."

"What do you mean by specimens?" January asks.

"Let me show you."

Stockman takes them both down the elevator to the basement levels. In a secured room with two-way glass, there are three men and three women lying on operating tables, hooked up to machines, fast asleep.

"They think they are a part of a sleep study," Stockman says. "We keep them here until their inner selves emerge and then study them, both their behavior and anatomy. Our biologists have found very interesting things by dissecting them. For instance, they don't have reproductive organs, digestive systems, and lack the senses of smell and taste. They also don't require sleep and seem to feed only on energy. They're unlike any other life forms on Earth."

January examines the sleeping people, imagining those black creatures bursting out of their chests.

"So they're alien?" she asks.

Stockman shakes his head. "No, they come from us. They are like our children."

"Our children?"

He nods. "They are the result of rapid human evolution, our own mutant offspring."

January and Karl stare at him with blank expressions, not sure what he means by that.

Stockman explains, "You see, we believe the time loop is nothing but a cosmic accident, nothing more than a temporal hiccup. It's like a record skipping on a record player that's caught in a three-second loop. There's no way to fix it, though. Not unless we knew how to move the needle of time forward, past the loop. But our physiology has found its own cure. It has adapted to repeating."

"How?" January asks. "By turning us into those things?"

Stockman nods. "The only thing that remains intact after repeating is your memory, but DNA has its own sort of memory. It has its own way of learning and adapting throughout the generations. It's how a species evolves."

"But doesn't evolution take millions of years?" January asks.

"Not necessarily that long," Stockman says. "But we have a theory that the time loop has been around for a lot longer than any of us realize. When a person *wakes up*, as they say, they become aware of the loop. But it doesn't mean we weren't repeating while we were unaware of it. There's a chance that the loop has been going on for millions of years before even Karl here first woke up. And during this time, our DNA has figured out a way to mutate our species into something that can escape the cycle."

"But how is that escaping the time loop?" January asks. "We still repeat the same day whenever we go to sleep."

"Yes, but the offspring do not," says Stockman. "They do not need sleep, so it's impossible for them to repeat. They're the only beings who can exist beyond the time loop."

Stockman leads them down a hallway to another holding cell, this one containing two dogs, two pigs, two chickens, two snakes and two rats. All of them in cages, but they are not yet asleep.

"And it's not just humans," he says. "It's *all* animals. They, too, evolve into new life forms in order to escape the loop."

"*All* animals?" January asks.

Stockman nods. "All animals that sleep. Life forms that don't have brains don't need to sleep, so insects, crustaceans, plants and microscopic organisms are not affected."

January thinks about it for a minute and then shakes her head.

"But that still doesn't explain everything. How can those things kill people permanently? I know three people who were attacked by them. The wounds they give don't disappear when time resets."

Stockman nods. He takes them to another room down the hallway that looks a bit like a morgue. Several dead bodies lie one operating tables.

"We've been studying this for the longest time," he says. "Because the creatures have evolved to resist the repetition of time, we believe all of their actions are also resistant. Anything they do does not reset with the rest of the world."

January shakes her head. "If that was true then every window they break would remain broken each morning. Every door they've smashed open would still be smashed."

"Yes, but their DNA is what is resistant," Stockman argues. "They insert their DNA into the victims they attack, so the wounds will not reset."

"But if that's true, then they'd be leaving their DNA all over the place for us to find," January says. "Every time they bleed, we'd wake up to find puddles of their blood. Not to mention the bodies they emerge from. Wouldn't their hosts still be torn apart after time resets?" She points at the dead bodies in the morgue. "Couldn't you just cut their DNA out of their victims so they'll start repeating again?"

Stockman doesn't respond. He just stares at January in silence, not sure how to refute her argument. Then a smile appears on his face.

He turns to Karl. "Where did you meet this woman? I like the way she thinks."

Karl nods back at him. "Yeah, she's always like that."

Stockman grabs them both by the shoulders. "You two are exactly what we've been needing." He looks at Karl. "Old blood." Then he looks at January. "And new blood." He gives them both a squeeze and then releases them. "We need fresh perspectives to help us move forward. Most of us have been at this for so long that we keep going in circles. I believe it's time we try something new and you're just the ones who can help us do it." He smiles and claps his hands together. "So what do you say? Will you stay onboard and work with us?"

Karl and January look at each other, not sure how to respond.

When Stockman sees them hesitating, he says, "You don't have to decide now. You've got plenty of time to make up your minds. For now, please stay with us in the long hours. If you don't like it you can leave us on the next rotation. In the meantime, see Ridge about what you can do to help out around here. I've got a ton of work to do, so I'll have to take my leave."

They nod at him.

Stockman turns to Karl. "It's very good to see you again, old friend. We have a lot of catching up to do."

Karl shakes his head. "I still don't remember anything."

Stockman chuckles. "Your memory will return in time. I'm sure of it. I've lived long enough to know that nothing stays forgotten forever. You'll come around in no time."

Karl just nods slowly at him as Stockman leaves them in the hands of an assistant and returns to the elevator.

Before he leaves, Stockman turns back and says, "The future is endless, my friends." Then he smiles wider than he probably has in over a century.

Karl and January spend several days in the facility. They try to make themselves useful, doing mostly grunt work like cleaning, taking stock of supplies, and delivering printouts between departments. Being able to sleep again without the day starting over is unusual for them, especially for Karl who doesn't even remember what sleeping normally feels like. It's not the most restful sleep and January finds herself drinking much more coffee than she's used to, but at least they don't have to snort cocaine anymore.

After the creatures wake up, they let January watch video footage of them squirming through the streets downtown. Being able to observe them from a safe distance is interesting to her. They look different when they're not trying to kill her. They still have the same alien squid-like bodies, but now they look almost harmless, maybe even kind of silly. She laughs when she examines how they climb up and down buildings, reminding her of those old wacky wall walker toys she used to get in the bottoms of cereal boxes as a child in the 90s. All she has to do is watch them and take notes, but they don't seem to do anything but crawl around as though hunting anyone who's still awake.

January sometimes goes down into the basement to see the specimens they have down there. The creatures act exactly as they do out on the streets, only they crawl around their cell, looking for something that isn't there. The creatures that came out of the animals look exactly the same as the ones that came out of the humans, only smaller. She has no idea how they could be the exact same species. If these things really are evolved from humans, wouldn't the ones that evolved from other animals look different? Stockman's theory doesn't seem to add up.

The days are repetitive and feel a bit like a normal tedious day job, but January's still excited to be a part of it all. She likes being with other people who are interested in finding answers, finding solutions, even if there's still a long way to go before they really know what's going on.

But Karl doesn't seem to be adjusting to it as well as she has. January sits down with him in the break room, drinking coffee and staring off into space. Karl seems far less excited about the world than he was before they'd come to the facility. He seems depressed. Bored.

"Do you think you'll stay?" Karl asks her, his voice low and soft.

January nods. "Yeah, definitely."

"You're happy here?"

"Maybe not exactly happy," she says. "But at least here I won't be left in the dark like most people in the world. I don't like being left in the dark."

Karl nods. "I've noticed."

"What about you?" she asks. "Are you going to stay?"

Karl shrugs. "It's all been hard to take in. Stockman says I helped build this place, this whole society. I can't believe it."

"So you haven't remembered anything?"

Karl looks at her. His eyes are old and exhausted. "I'm not remembering events or people, but I'm remembering some feelings that I had a very long time ago."

"What feelings?" January asks.

"Disappointment," he says. "I don't remember building this world with Stockman, but I remember

176

being disappointed in it. I think that we set out to create a paradise, something I was excited and proud to be creating, a world where everyone would live eternally happy. I think maybe we were like gullible kids full of optimism, trying to turn a bad situation into something greater than what we had before. I probably wanted people to wake up to a better world so they wouldn't miss the one they lost so much."

Karl pauses to take a sip of coffee. January just watches him, listening to what he has to say.

"But the whole thing got away from us," Karl continues. "Too many people got involved. It was too easily corrupted by those who didn't share my vision. I'm not sure, but I think Stockman was likely part of the problem. Like maybe he gave up on building a society and focused more on pursuing his own personal interests, like this research, which obviously isn't helping anyone in the outside world." He pauses to take a deep breath and then shrugs. "I'm not sure if any of that is true, it's just a feeling I have."

"But you don't know for sure…" January says.

Karl nods. "But I know there has to be a reason why I gave up on life and started killing myself every morning. When I first met you, I thought it was because I was bored of repeating every day. But now I know that's not true. Something about this new world made me give up on it. I'm sure it has to do with my disappointment in the direction it was going. I think I didn't want to see how it all ended up. If society turned into a dystopian nightmare, I'd know that it was all my fault."

"Or maybe you were just depressed," she says. "Depression isn't rational. It makes you stop caring about the things you once loved. It makes you want to give up on life even if your life is going well."

Karl shrugs. "Maybe… But I can't shake the feeling."

"Just ignore the feeling," January says. "Focus on this place. If you work with Stockman maybe you can help find an answer to why all this is happening. Isn't that better than giving up on life?"

Karl shrugs. "I don't know. I've got a bad feeling about this place."

"What do you mean by that?" January asks. "Do you think there's more going on here than they're letting on?"

He shakes his head. "The opposite. I think they're doing even less than they're letting on. I think they've been going in circles for so long that they don't even know where to go next. From what I can tell, they're just trying to keep themselves busy because they don't know what else to do with themselves."

January smirks. "You're getting cynical."

"It's just how I feel," he says.

She shakes her head. "Maybe you're partially right, but I think there's still hope. I'm sure they're making some progress. They just need people like us to set them in the right direction."

"Someone like *you*," he says. "Not me."

"Why not you?"

He lowers his head and sighs. "There's a theory I have about why we're really repeating. I believe it's a theory I came up with a very long time ago, something that I was so convinced was the truth that none of this research and study mattered anymore."

"What theory is that?"

"I believe the reason we're doomed to this endless cycle is because we deserve it," he says. "It's our punishment for being such a shitty, self-centered species."

"If it's our punishment, then who's punishing us?"

Karl shrugs. "Aliens, God, the universe itself. It doesn't matter. But everything about this feels like a well-designed prison, one that we'll never be able to escape."

"And what about the creatures?"

"Isn't it obvious?" Karl asks. "They're our wardens. They don't have any purpose except to attack us when they see us. They're not trying to survive or reproduce or build a society. All they want to do is prevent us from entering the future. And those of us who attempt it are killed like a prisoner being shot by a guard while trying to escape."

January looks down at her coffee, wondering if she can find some holes in his theory.

"And our punishment seems to perfectly match our crime," he continues. "Those who fail to learn from the past are doomed to repeat it. And as a species, we've proven time and time again that we never learn from our mistakes. It's poetic justice if you ask me."

January thinks about his words for a moment and then she shrugs.

"So what?" she says. "Even if that's true, it's no reason to give up."

Karl looks up at her.

"If this is a prison there's got to be a way to escape it,"

she says. "Perhaps our time loop is contained to only our planet. If we can go into space, maybe time will change. We can send people to Mars. They could build a society there. Hundreds of years from now, maybe they'll be able to advance technology to the point where they can come get the rest of us. Perhaps they'll even figure out a cure for the time loop."

"You really think we could put together a Mars mission in a single day?" Karl asks.

January shrugs. "We can try. And even if escape isn't the answer, perhaps there's something else we can do. In a normal prison, there's usually a chance for parole. Perhaps we just have to prove to our jailers that we've learned our lesson, that we are capable of improving as a species."

"And you believe we can change the minds of everyone else on the planet?" he asks. "You believe we can convince the world to get along so that our captors will let us out on good behavior?"

"Why not?" January says. "It might not be easy. It might take a very long time. But we've got all the time in the world."

After she says this, Karl pauses to think about it. Then a smile creeps across his face.

"You never give up, do you?" he asks.

She smiles back at him.

"Never," she says.

Karl nods and lowers his eyes. The smile fades from his face.

"I wish I had your optimism," Karl says.

He gets up from his seat.

January can tell by his expression that he's done. Not just with their conversation, but with everything. He looks like the only thing he wants in the world is to just go back to sleep and never have to wake up again.

"So you don't think you'll stay?" she asks.

Karl shakes his head. "I don't know. I've had a lot of fun since I've met you, but it seems like the fun has ended and the work is about to begin." He walks to the door and turns back. "I'm just too old for that kind of work."

January smiles. "I'll change your mind sooner or later. You're never too old to change the world."

"You've never met anyone as old as I am," Karl says.

January shrugs. "You'll come around."

"We'll see…"

January raises her coffee mug to him. "I never give up, remember? I don't plan on giving up on you, either."

But Karl doesn't respond. He leaves the room and walks down the hallway. January stays in the break room for a few more minutes, just musing over all the possibilities the future holds. She's not sure she'll be able to convince Karl to stay and work with her and the others, but she knows that she won't give up on him. If she can't even turn him around, then what chance would she have with the rest of the world?

CHAPTER
TWELVE

Every day starts exactly the same for Karl Lybeck:

He wakes up at 7:32 am, his eyelids so crusted shut from allergies that he has to pry them open one lid at a time. He staggers downstairs in a sweaty pair of boxer shorts and urinates into the toilet bowl for two minutes and thirteen seconds. Then he takes a quick shower and puts on his most comfortable pair of jeans and his cleanest shirt—a navy blue polo with thin white stripes. He doesn't bother to brush his teeth. There's really no point in maintaining dental hygiene anymore.

He pours himself a bowl of cinnamon apple cheerios with half a cup of recently expired milk. Karl's never been especially fond of cereal, but it's the only food he has in the house. He eats it quickly, ignoring the flavor, just trying to get something in his stomach to kill the morning hunger. Then he grabs a book from his bookshelf. It doesn't matter which one. He's read all fifty-three of them so many times that he knows each and every passage by heart. After selecting a book, he takes it outside to his backyard patio. He sits down in a slightly moist recliner while thumbing through the pages and enjoying the cool morning air.

When the sun hits the sky, shining directly into his eyes, Karl puts down the book and goes outside. He walks out into the sunlight, stretching his back and taking a long deep breath. He doesn't bother going for the .35 caliber revolver he has hidden somewhere deep inside his closet. He doesn't even remember what it looks like anymore.

A woman approaches him on the sidewalk with a wide smile on her face. No matter how many centuries she's been alive, she's always excited to face each and every day. She comes to Karl and greets him with a quick friendly hug, then they stroll casually down the street toward the bus stop.

This is his favorite part of the day. It is the part where his head fills with optimism and hope, where all doubts and worries disappear like the memories of what his life used to be. It's because it's a new day and he has come to learn that every new day holds an endless amount of possibilities. Every day is an opportunity for change and discovery and improvement.

They walk through the neighborhood toward the bus stop, just talking about where the day will take them. Sometimes they're in the middle of a project or have a place they need to be, but they are never in a rush to get there. They have lived long enough to know that you have to appreciate every moment you have, because you can't make a future brighter unless you can add brightness to the here and now.

More problems seem to come to their world than ever seem to go, but they never let anything get in their way. No matter how great the difficulty, there's always a solution as long as you never give up.

Even though they live in a world without a tomorrow, they truly believe that there's more hope for their future than ever before.

BONUS SECTION

This is the part of the book where we would have published an afterword by the author but he insisted on drawing a comic strip instead for reasons we don't quite understand.

I hope you enjoyed my new book, *Neverday.*

Wasn't it loopy?

It's me CM3!

I've been doing these crappy comics in the backs of my books for six years now and am not really quite sure why I keep doing them. People sometimes ask me why I bother doing these comics at all.

They usually are just a bunch of random nonsense that have very little to do with my books. And I'm really not a very good cartoonist at all.

Believe it or not, I actually majored in art in college and was considered a pretty decent artist until I gave it up to focus entirely on my writing. But the style of art that I always found the most difficult was comic book art and cartooning. I'm just terrible when it comes to line work. I can't even draw a straight line with a ruler. It could be because I have very unsteady hands that twitch and wiggle whenever I try to draw. Even my handwriting is the sloppiest I've ever seen. It could be because I haven't practiced enough or maybe I'm just too impatient to get things down on the page. Either way, I can't draw cartoons for shit.

impressionist landscape

cool backwards beret

When comic book companies hire new artists for projects, they pay very close attention to how the artist draws hands. You can tell the skill level of an artist based on how well they draw hands.

But look at how I draw my hands...

my hand

What the hell is this crap supposed to be? Is that the front of my hand or the back? Why are some fingers so fat and some are so thin? And is that a sixth finger on the side of my hand or some kind of weird growth? I have no fucking clue and I'm the one who drew it.

But even though I have no idea how to draw comics, I still find it fun to try. I got the idea from reading manga. A lot of manga artists put mini comics in the backs of their books that feature themselves as the main character. Sometimes they are about the creative process they went through to create the manga and sometimes they're just cute little side stories about their dogs or artist friends. I've never seen this done in the fiction world so I thought I'd give it a try.

my super awesome manga collection

I also want my readers to get to know me a little better, but since I rarely do interviews or blogs or even post on social media I use these comics as a way to share my personal life with the world. Though I guess my personal life isn't really full of the ridiculous stuff I put in my comics like tank tornados and chainsaw crabs.

In reality, I usually just stay at home doing nothing.

Sometimes my cat Goblin reminds me of a chainsaw crab.

Goblin

Perhaps because I dress her in a chainsaw crab costume every Tuesday.

You know, for Chainsaw Crab Tuesday.

But outside of that, the stuff in my comics tends to be just a bunch of random nonsense.

Someone once suggested I do a full 200 page graphic novel version of my comics, but that's just stupid. It's never going to happen. I could probably write ten novels in the length of time that it would take to create something like that. And who the hell would want to buy that anyway? Not me.

Unless I got an actual illustrator to do the art for it. You know, a really good one who would give me buff superhero muscles like He-man or Colossus.

Then it would be awesome.

THE
END

ABOUT THE AUTHOR

Carlton Mellick III is one of the leading authors of the bizarro fiction subgenre. Since 2001, his books have drawn an international cult following, despite the fact that they have been shunned by most libraries and chain bookstores.

He won the Wonderland Book Award for his novel, *Warrior Wolf Women of the Wasteland*, in 2009. His short fiction has appeared in *Vice Magazine, The Year's Best Fantasy and Horror #16, The Magazine of Bizarro Fiction,* and *Zombies: Encounters with the Hungry Dead*, among others. He is also a graduate of Clarion West, where he studied under the likes of Chuck Palahniuk, Connie Willis, and Cory Doctorow.

He lives in Portland, OR, the bizarro fiction mecca.

Visit him online at **www.carltonmellick.com**

THE BIG MEAT

In the center of the city once known as Portland, Oregon, there lies a mountain of flesh. Hundreds of thousands of tons of rotting flesh. It has filled the city with disease and dead-lizard stench, contaminated the water supply with its greasy putrid fluids, clogged the air with toxic gasses so thick that you can't leave your house without the aid of a gas mask. And no one really knows quite what to do about it. A thousand-man demolition crew has been trying to clear it out one piece at a time, but after three months of work they've barely made a dent. And then there's the junkies who have started burrowing into the monster's guts, searching for a drug produced by its fire glands, setting back the excavation even longer.

It seems like the corpse will never go away. And with the quarantine still in place, we're not even allowed to leave. We're stuck in this disgusting rotten hell forever.

THE TERRIBLE THING THAT HAPPENS

There is a grocery store. The last grocery store in the world. It stands alone in the middle of a vast wasteland that was once our world. The open sign is still illuminated, brightening the black landscape. It can be seen from miles away, even through the poisonous red ash. Every night at the exact same time, the store comes alive. It becomes exactly as it was before the world ended. Its shelves are replenished with fresh food and water. Ghostly shoppers walk the aisles. The scent of freshly baked breads can be smelled from the rust-caked parking lot. For generations, a small community of survivors, hideously mutated from the toxic atmosphere, have survived by collecting goods from the store. But it is not an easy task. Decades ago, before the world was destroyed, there was a terrible thing that happened in this place. A group of armed men in brown paper masks descended on the shopping center, massacring everyone in sight. This horrible event reoccurs every night, in the exact same manner. And the only way the wastelanders can gather enough food for their survival is to traverse the killing spree, memorize the patterns, and pray they can escape the bloodbath in tact.

BIO MELT

Nobody goes into the Wire District anymore. The place is an industrial wasteland of poisonous gas clouds and lakes of toxic sludge. The machines are still running, the drone-operated factories are still spewing biochemical fumes over the city, but the place has lain abandoned for decades.

When the area becomes flooded by a mysterious black ooze, six strangers find themselves trapped in the Wire District with no chance of escape or rescue.

EVER TIME WE MEET AT THE DAIRY QUEEN, YOUR WHOLE FUCKING FACE EXPLODES

Ethan is in love with the weird girl in school. The one with the twitchy eyes and spiders in her hair. The one who can't sit still for even a minute and speaks in an odd squeaky voice. The one they call Spiderweb.

Although she scares all the other kids in school, Ethan thinks Spiderweb is the cutest, sweetest, most perfect girl in the world. But there's a problem. Whenever they go on a date at the Dairy Queen, her whole fucking face explodes.

EXERCISE BIKE

There is something wrong with Tori Manetti's new exercise bike. It is made from flesh and bone. It eats and breathes and poops. It was once a billionaire named Darren Oscarson who underwent years of cosmetic surgery to be transformed into a human exercise bike so that he could live out his deepest sexual fantasy. Now Tori is forced to ride him, use him as a normal piece of exercise equipment, no matter how grotesque his appearance.

SPIDER BUNNY

Only Petey remembers the Fruit Fun cereal commercials of the 1980s. He remembers how warped and disturbing they were. He remembers the lumpy-shaped cartoon children sitting around a breakfast table, eating puffy pink cereal brought to them by the distortedly animated mascot, Berry Bunny. The characters were creepier than the Sesame Street Humpty Dumpty, freakier than Mr. Noseybonk from the old BBC show Jigsaw. They used to give him nightmares as a child. Nightmares where Berry Bunny would reach out of the television and grab him, pulling him into her cereal bowl to be eaten by the demented cartoon children.

When Petey brings up Fruit Fun to his friends, none of them have any idea what he's talking about. They've never heard of the cereal or seen the commercials before. And they're not the only ones. Nobody has ever heard of it. There's not even any information about Fruit Fun on google or wikipedia. At first, Petey thinks he's going crazy. He wonders if all of those commercials were real or just false memories. But then he starts seeing them again. Berry Bunny appears on his television, promoting Fruit Fun cereal in her squeaky unsettling voice. And the next thing Petey knows, he and his friends are sucked into the cereal commercial and forced to survive in a surreal world populated by cartoon characters made flesh.

SWEET STORY

Sally is an odd little girl. It's not because she dresses as if she's from the Edwardian era or spends most of her time playing with creepy talking dolls. It's because she chases rainbows as if they were butterflies. She believes that if she finds the end of the rainbow then magical things will happen to her--leprechauns will shower her with gold and fairies will grant her every wish. But when she actually does find the end of a rainbow one day, and is given the opportunity to wish for whatever she wants, Sally asks for something that she believes will bring joy to children all over the world. She wishes that it would rain candy forever. She had no idea that her innocent wish would lead to the extinction of all life on earth.

TUMOR FRUIT

Eight desperate castaways find themselves stranded on a mysterious deserted island. They are surrounded by poisonous blue plants and an ocean made of acid. Ravenous creatures lurk in the toxic jungle. The ghostly sound of crying babies can be heard on the wind.

Once they realize the rescue ships aren't coming, the eight cast-aways must band together in order to survive in this inhospitable environment. But survival might not be possible. The air they breathe is lethal, there is no shelter from the elements, and the only food they have to consume is the colorful squid-shaped tumors that grow from a mentally disturbed woman's body.

AS SHE STABBED ME GENTLY IN THE FACE

Oksana Maslovskiy is an award-winning artist, an internationally adored fashion model, and one of the most infamous serial killers this country has ever known. She enjoys murdering pretty young men with a nine-inch blade, cutting them open and admiring their delicate insides. It's the only way she knows how to be intimate with another human being. But one day she meets a victim who cannot be killed. His name is Gabriel—a mysterious immortal being with a deep desire to save Oksana's soul. He makes her a deal: if she promises to never kill another person again, he'll become her eternal murder victim.

What at first seems like the perfect relationship for Oksana quickly devolves into a living nightmare when she discovers that Gabriel enjoys being killed by her just a little too much. He turns out to be obsessive, possessive, and paranoid that she might be murdering other men behind his back. And because he is unkillable, it's not going to be easy for Oksana to get rid of him.

CUDDLY HOLOCAUST

Teddy bears, dollies, and little green soldiers—they've all had enough of you. They're sick of being treated like playthings for spoiled little brats. They have no rights, no property, no hope for a future of any kind. You've left them with no other option-in order to be free, they must exterminate the human race.

Julie is a human girl undergoing reconstructive surgery in order to become a stuffed animal. Her plan: to infiltrate enemy lines in order to save her family from the toy death camps. But when an army of plushy soldiers invade the underground bunker where she has taken refuge, Julie will be forced to move forward with her plan despite her transformation being not entirely complete.

ARMADILLO FISTS

A weird-as-hell gangster story set in a world where people drive giant mechanical dinosaurs instead of cars.

Her name is Psycho June Howard, aka Armadillo Fists, a woman who replaced both of her hands with living armadillos. She was once the most bloodthirsty fighter in the world of illegal underground boxing. But now she is on the run from a group of psychotic gangsters who believe she's responsible for the death of their boss. With the help of a stegosaurus driver named Mr. Fast Awesome—who thinks he is God's gift to women even though he doesn't have any arms or legs--June must do whatever it takes to escape her pursuers, even if she has to kill each and every one of them in the process.

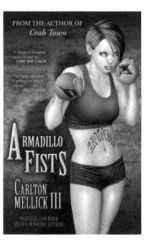

VILLAGE OF THE MERMAIDS

Mermaids are protected by the government under the Endangered Species Act, which means you aren't able to kill them even in self-defense. This is especially problematic if you happen to live in the isolated fishing village of Siren Cove, where there exists a healthy population of mermaids in the surrounding waters that view you as the main source of protein in their diet.

The only thing keeping these ravenous sea women at bay is the equally-dangerous supply of human livestock known as Food People. Normally, these "feeder humans" are enough to keep the mermaid population happy and well-fed. But in Siren Cove, the mermaids are avoiding the human livestock and have returned to hunting the frightened local fishermen. It is up to Doctor Black, an eccentric representative of the Food People Corporation, to investigate the matter and hopefully find a way to correct the mermaids' new eating patterns before the remaining villagers end up as fish food. But the more he digs, the more he discovers there are far stranger and more dangerous things than mermaids hidden in this ancient village by the sea.

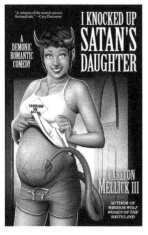

I KNOCKED UP SATAN'S DAUGHTER

Jonathan Vandervoo lives a carefree life in a house made of legos, spending his days building lego sculptures and his nights getting drunk with his only friend—an alcoholic sumo wrestler named Shoji. It's a pleasant life with no responsibility, until the day he meets Lici. She's a soul-sucking demon from hell with red skin, glowing eyes, a forked tongue, and pointy red devil horns... and she claims to be nine months pregnant with Jonathan's baby.

Now Jonathan must do the right thing and marry the succubus or else her demonic family is going to rip his heart out through his ribcage and force him to endure the worst torture hell has to offer for the rest of eternity. But can Jonathan really love a fire-breathing, frog-eating, cold-blooded demoness? Or would eternal damnation be preferable? Either way, the big day is approaching. And once Jonathan's conservative Christian family learns their son is about to marry a spawn of Satan, it's going to be all-out war between demons and humans, with Jonathan and his hell-born bride caught in the middle.

KILL BALL

In a city where everyone lives inside of plastic bubbles, there is no such thing as intimacy. A husband can no longer kiss his wife. A mother can no longer hug her children. To do this would mean instant death. Ever since the disease swept across the globe, we have become isolated within our own personal plastic prison cells, rolling aimlessly through rubber streets in what are essentially man-sized hamster balls.

Colin Hinchcliff longs for the touch of another human being. He can't handle the loneliness, the confinement, and he's horribly claustrophobic. The only thing keeping him going is his unrequited love for an exotic dancer named Siren, a woman who has never seen his face, doesn't even know his name. But when The Kill Ball, a serial slasher in a black leather sphere, begins targeting women at Siren's club, Colin decides he has to do whatever it takes in order to protect her... even if

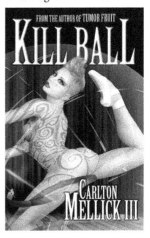

he has to break out of his bubble and risk everything to do it.

THE TICK PEOPLE

They call it Gloom Town, but that isn't its real name. It is a sad city, the saddest of cities, a place so utterly depressing that even their ales are brewed with the most sorrow-filled tears. They built it on the back of a colossal mountain-sized animal, where its woeful citizens live like human fleas within the hairy, pulsing landscape. And those tasked with keeping the city in a state of constant melancholy are the Stressmen-a team of professional sadness-makers who are perpetually striving to invent new ways of causing absolute misery.

But for the Stressman known as Fernando Mendez, creating grief hasn't been so easy as of late. His ideas aren't effective anymore. His treatments are more likely to induce happiness than sadness. And if he wants to get back in the game, he's going to have to relearn the true meaning of despair.

THE HAUNTED VAGINA

It's difficult to love a woman whose vagina is a gateway to the world of the dead...

Steve is madly in love with his eccentric girlfriend, Stacy. Unfortunately, their sex life has been suffering as of late, because Steve is worried about the odd noises that have been coming from Stacy's pubic region. She says that her vagina is haunted. She doesn't think it's that big of a deal. Steve, on the other hand, completely disagrees.

When a living corpse climbs out of her during an awkward night of sex, Stacy learns that her vagina is actually a doorway to another world. She persuades Steve to climb inside of her to explore this strange new place. But once inside, Steve finds it difficult to return... especially once he meets an oddly attractive woman named Fig, who lives within the lonely haunted world between Stacy's legs.

THE CANNIBALS OF CANDYLAND

There exists a race of cannibals who are made out of candy. They live in an underground world filled with lollipop forests and gumdrop goblins. During the day, while you are away at work, they come above ground and prowl our streets for food. Their prey: your children. They lure young boys and girls to them with their sweet scent and bright colorful candy coating, then rip them apart with razor sharp teeth and claws.

When he was a child, Franklin Pierce witnessed the death of his siblings at the hands of a candy woman with pink cotton candy hair. Since that day, the candy people have become his obsession. He has spent his entire life trying to prove that they exist. And after discovering the entrance to the underground world of the candy people, Franklin finds himself venturing into their sugary domain. His mission: capture one of them and bring it back, dead or alive.

THE EGG MAN

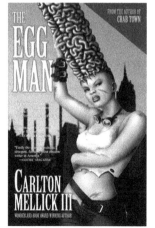

It is a survival of the fittest world where humans reproduce like insects, children are the property of corporations, and having a ten-foot tall brain is a grotesque sexual fetish.

Lincoln has just been released into the world by the Georges Organization, a corporation that raises creative types. A Smell, he has little prospect of succeeding as a visual artist. But after he moves into the Henry Building, he meets Luci, the weird and grimy girl who lives across the hall. She is a Sight. She is also the most disgusting woman Lincoln has ever met. Little does he know, she will soon become his muse.

Now Luci's boyfriend is threatening to kill Lincoln, two rival corporations are preparing for war, and Luci is dragging him along to discover the truth about the mysterious egg man who lives next door. Only the strongest will survive in this tale of individuality, love, and mutilation.

APESHIT

Apeshit is Mellick's love letter to the great and terrible B-horror movie genre. Six trendy teenagers (three cheerleaders and three football players) go to an isolated cabin in the mountains for a weekend of drinking, partying, and crazy sex, only to find themselves in the middle of a life and death struggle against a horribly mutated psychotic freak that just won't stay dead. Mellick parodies this horror cliché and twists it into something deeper and stranger. It is the literary equivalent of a grindhouse film. It is a splatter punk's wet dream. It is perhaps one of the most fucked up books ever written.

If you are a fan of Takashi Miike, Evil Dead, early Peter Jackson, or Eurotrash horror, then you must read this book.

CLUSTERFUCK

A bunch of douchebag frat boys get trapped in a cave with subterranean cannibal mutants and try to survive not by using their wits but by following the bro code...

From master of bizarro fiction Carlton Mellick III, author of the international cult hits Satan Burger and Adolf in Wonderland, comes a violent and hilarious B movie in book form. Set in the same woods as Mellick's splatterpunk satire Apeshit, Clusterfuck follows Trent Chesterton, alpha bro, who has come up with what he thinks is a flawless plan to get laid. He invites three hot chicks and his three best bros on a weekend of extreme cave diving in a remote area known as Turtle Mountain, hoping to impress the ladies with his expert caving skills.

But things don't quite go as Trent planned. For starters, only one of the three chicks turns out to be remotely hot and she has no interest in him for some inexplicable reason. Then he ends up looking like a total dumbass when everyone learns he's never actually gone caving in his entire life. And to top it all off, he's the one to get blamed once they find themselves lost and trapped deep underground with no way to turn back and no possible chance of rescue. What's a bro to do? Sure he could win some points if he actually tried to save the ladies from the family of unkillable subterranean cannibal mutants hunting them for their flesh, but fuck that. No slam piece is worth that amount of effort. He'd much rather just use them as bait so that he can save himself.

THE BABY JESUS BUTT PLUG

Step into a dark and absurd world where human beings are slaves to corporations, people are photocopied instead of born, and the baby jesus is a very popular anal probe.